Midnight Mystery

★ ★ ★ ★ ★

Winnie

The Horse Gentler   4

Tyndale House Publishers, Inc.
Carol Stream, Illinois

Midnight Mystery

DANDI DALEY MACKALL

Visit Tyndale online at www.tyndale.com.

You can contact Dandi Daley Mackall through her website at
www.dandibooks.com.

TYNDALE and Tyndale's quill logo are trademarks of Tyndale House
Publishers, Inc.

Midnight Mystery

Designed by Jacqueline L. Nuñez

Edited by Ramona Cramer Tucker

For manufacturing information regarding this product, please call
1-800-323-9400.

For information about special discounts for bulk purchases, please
contact Tyndale House Publishers at csresponse@tyndale.com, or call
1-800-323-9400.

ISBN 978-0-8423-5545-2, mass paper

Printed in the United States of America

24 23 22 21 20 19 18
16 15 14 13 12 11 10

To Sharon Yorks, along with
Russell and Doris Smith—
Thanks for your help with circus details
and for sharing your circus
experiences with me!

Quit horsing around, Nickers! Bow!" I tickled
my white Arabian's belly and tried to rein in my
famous temper.

I love my horse more than anything, and
Nickers is a fast learner. I'd taught her half a
dozen tricks in under two weeks. But she can
be as stubborn as I am. We'd been training all
Saturday in the pasture behind my barn. Dusk
had moved in on a breeze that shook the last
fall leaves off oaks and poplars, and Nickers
hadn't bowed once for me.

I'd only had time to teach my horse tricks
because I was temporarily out of problem
horses to train. When my dad moved my sister,
Lizzy, and me to Ashland, Ohio, two big things
happened. I got my own horse, Nickers. And I

became Winnie the Horse Gentler because I was the only one who could gentle my Arabian.

I'd learned all about horses from my mom. Mom used to say I would have made a great horse. It's true—I'm better with horses than people.

Back in Wyoming, Mom had her own ranch. She'd earned a reputation for "gentling" horses instead of "breaking" them. When she died two years ago, Dad sold everything and drove Lizzy and me eastward. But he couldn't settle down, and I'd spent fifth and sixth grades in the *I* states, zigzagging from Illinois to Indiana to Iowa.

Ashland, Ohio, had shown up like an answer to a prayer nobody prayed. We'd been here four months, and I'd already started seventh grade and gentled several horses. Plus I had a part-time job at Pat's Pets, answering horse e-mail questions on the Pet Help Line. I was still boarding Towaco, my friend Hawk's Appaloosa, but I'd returned my last problem horse, a hunter, to her owner. And I wasn't expecting more clients until spring.

I blew into Nickers' nostrils, a horse greeting to let her know I wasn't really angry about her not bowing. We were friends training each other. She blew back, saying she understood.

I returned to a trick she'd mastered. "Nickers, how many days until our performance?" I'd trained her by tickling behind her front leg. Now all I had to do was crook my finger.

Nickers pawed the ground with each bend of my finger: *one, two, three, four, five, six.* Six days till November 12, Mom's birthday.

Pictures of past birthdays flashed through my mind. We always watched *Lady and the Tramp* in the morning and ate spaghetti for lunch. Then, in the afternoon, Mom always put on a horse show for Dad, Lizzy, and me.

My brain had snapped detailed photos of Mom's horse shows. Mom used to say she'd known from the day I was born that I had a photographic memory. Dad had teased her about it until they had me tested and found out she was right. I can't control the "camera" in my head, so lots of the pictures are things I wish hadn't been stored, like the ones of the car accident that killed my mom.

But I was grateful for each birthday picture that popped into my head as I scratched Nickers' neck. I could see Mom, with dark hair and freckles just like mine, smiling from the back of her bowing buckskin. Another picture showed a black Mustang lying flat on the ground with Mom lying beside her. The pictures rolled at their own speed, ending with the Quarter Horse Mom had taught to do everything except cook breakfast.

Then a different picture exploded inside my head: Mom proudly showing us her birthday cake. Every year green icing spelled out the same verse from the book of Hebrews: *Jesus Christ is the same yesterday, today, and forever.*

I stroked Nickers' white fuzz, the beginnings of her winter coat, and let the green letters fade in my mind. So many things *weren't* the same. Mom was dead. Dad had changed from an insurance boss to an odd-job handyman and part-time inventor. Even Lizzy was changing, getting more involved in school stuff.

Dad and Lizzy and I needed this birthday to pull us back. For the first two birthdays after Mom died, we'd watched the movie and eaten the spaghetti. This time I wanted to surprise them and have the horse show. Nickers and I had exactly six days, starting tomorrow, to learn to bow.

"Cool."

I jumped, even though I should have been

4

used to the way Catman Coolidge can sneak up on a person. "Nickers," I said, not turning around, "is it rude to sneak up on people?" I pointed to the ground, our signal for yes.

Nickers bobbed her beautiful head in a dramatic yes.

"Far out!" Catman exclaimed.

I grinned at him. He was wearing a tie-dyed shirt, a denim vest, and striped bell-bottoms fraying over the tops of his moccasins. With his wire-rimmed glasses, he seems older than an eighth-grader. And he looks like the longhaired protesters and hippies in the Vietnam chapter of my history book.

"Nickers, is Catman as smart as you?" I moved my hand to her withers.

Nickers picked up my withers cue and shook her head *no*.

"Colonel sees that, he'll make you groove with his circus," Catman warned.

"Can't believe I'm finally going to meet your great-grandfather!" I'd heard stories about "the Colonel." He was a World War II hero who now ran a traveling circus. And he was bringing his whole circus to Ashland for the season's last two performances. "Can you get Lizzy and me tickets for Thursday night?" Friday night, the last show, would probably be better. But that was Mom's birthday, and I'd be putting on my own horse show.

I unhooked Nickers' leadrope, but she stayed put. "Catman, do you know the circus people with the horse acts? Could you ask them how they get their horses to bow?"

"Ask them yourself." Catman's Siamese-blue eyes twinkled.

"I need to know before Thursday. Didn't you tell me they'd be performing in a different town every night on the way to Ashland?" I asked.

"Colonel Coolidge's Traveling Circus never rests," he answered. "They're in Loudonville tonight." Catman turned toward our house. "Let's split."

I stared after Catman. "Tonight?" Loudonville was only a few miles away, but how were we supposed to get there?

"The Barkers are coming by!" he hollered, evidently reading my thoughts. He stopped to pet my barn cat, Nelson. "Barker's in the show."

"*Our* Barker?" Eddy Barker's in seventh grade like I am. He loves dogs as much as Catman loves cats and I love horses.

I kissed Nickers and followed Catman, dodging the junk and machine parts that littered our lawn, stuff my dad calls "works-in-progress."

"What's Barker do in the circus?"

"Dogs." Catman reached the front steps and opened the door for me.

I ran inside and found Dad kneeling in front of a weird metal box on the kitchen floor. "Dad, is Lizzy back from her lizard hunt yet?" In her four months in Ashland, my sister had set up a farm for lizard refugees. She knows more about bugs, reptiles, and amphibians than any teacher I've ever had. Lizzy also babysits Barker's five little brothers. I knew they'd want her to come with us.

"Lizzy? Here?" Dad twisted two wires together. He wouldn't have known if Godzilla were here. Our mom had done such a great job as mom that Dad was still learning how to be a dad. He reminded me of a Saddle Horse Mom had bred in Wyoming. For a week after the mare foaled, she seemed surprised by motherhood. You could tell she loved her foal. She just didn't know what to do with it.

"Never mind, Dad." I checked all four rooms of our rental house, ending back in the kitchen.

Catman was holding a foil strip while Dad screwed it to the box. "Did you know . . ." Dad grunted between turns of the screwdriver ". . . that the microwave . . . was invented after a researcher . . . walked by a radar tube and his candy bar melted in his pocket?"

I stared at the box contraption. "You're re-inventing the microwave?"

Dad patted the box as if it were his third child. "Winnie, you're looking at a cold-a-wave! If I can get this to work, you'll be able to put in a warm glass of water and in seconds take out a cold glass of water!"

Note to self: Tell Dad to invent the ice cube.

Actually, I was kind of proud of Dad for inventing stuff—except when his inventions embarrassed me, like the backward bike I had to ride to school or the shoe alarm that accidentally got our school a free fire drill. Dad had even gotten up enough nerve a while ago to enter an invention contest. He'd never be famous, but playing with his inventions made him happy and kept us in Ashland.

A horn beeped outside.

"Dad, Barkers are here! Okay if I go to the circus with them—in Loudonville?"

"Circus?" Dad stuck his head inside the cold-a-wave.

"Elephants, horses, clowns . . . ?" I prodded.

"Have fun!" Dad shouted, but from inside the box it sounded more like *harumm*.

I followed Catman to the door. "Bye, Dad!" I shouted back.

He didn't answer. Probably still had his head in the cold-a-wave. In Wyoming, Dad had gone to his office in Laramie six days a week, but I couldn't remember saying good-bye to him even once. I think he left before I got up in the morning. Sometimes he came back after I'd gone to bed. Even if we did say good-bye, I don't think we ever hugged. And after Mom's accident, I know we didn't. Dad and I barely touched, apologizing for it when we did.

But things were getting better.

"Be there in a minute, Catman!" I ran back to Dad. I'm short, and Dad's tall, so with him kneeling before the cold-a-wave, our heads were even. I hugged him. His curly, black hair scratched my cheek. "Bye, Dad."

Dad sat back on his heels. The corners of his mouth curled up, and his Adam's apple jerked. "Bye, Winnie. Thanks."

I turned and ran to the Barker van, grateful for the chilly wind on my face.

"Where's Lizzy?" Mark Barker demanded as I climbed into the middle seat next to Catman. Mark is seven and a coltlike version of his stocky dad. Mr. Barker used to play football for Ashland University, where he and Mrs. Barker teach now.

I had to step over Mark's chocolate Lab and Johnny's black-and-tan coon dog, both strapped into little dog seat belts on the floor, Dad's invention. William's collie and Luke's Chihuahua barked from the backseat. Barker had rescued strays and trained one for each of his brothers.

Johnny, Luke, and William, the three youngest Barkers, fired questions at me like it was my fault Lizzy wasn't there.

"Guys!" Mrs. Barker called back. She and Granny Barker took up the front seat, with Matthew in between them. Mrs. Barker was the designated driver of the Barkers' yellow van, which looked more like a school bus. She's tall, with short, black hair and a deeper brown skin than most of her kids. "I think what you gentlemen meant to say was 'Hello, Winnie and

Catman. Glad *you're* here.'" She grinned at us in the rearview mirror, and I caught her winking at her husband in the backseat.

Sometimes I try to imagine what breeds people would be if they turned into horses. Mrs. Barker might be a graceful Tennessee Walker. Mr. Barker would make a good-natured Percheron. The boys are wild Mustangs, except for Barker, who's a steady Morgan.

"So tell me about Barker's act," I asked as we left Ashland, heading south.

Mr. Barker leaned forward, where he was wedged between kid car seats. "Eddy's a clown!"

"A dog-trainer clown!" Mark added, pride pouring out of each word. "And he's using Irene!" He stroked his Lab.

"And Chico!" Luke shouted.

"Macho gonna be star!" four-year-old Johnny announced. He glanced at William, the only Barker younger than he is. "William's dog, too!"

"Congratulations!" I couldn't help envying the Barker kids, with *two* great parents. I shook it off and turned to Matthew. At age nine, he's the only Barker who doesn't have a permanent smile. His bulldog was the only absent Barker dog. "Where's Bull, Matthew?"

Matthew Barker remained face-front, arms crossed.

The car grew silent.

"Matthew's dog . . . has a mind of his own," Mr. Barker offered. "I'm sure he'll come around before the Ashland circus. This has all happened rather fast. Two clowns got the flu. Trixie, the main trick dog, just had puppies. So the Colonel asked Barker to fill in, probably to get on Granny's good side."

Catman leaned in. "The Colonel digs Granny Barker."

Granny Barker kept staring out the window as if she didn't even hear the rest of us. Barker said that sometimes she probably doesn't know what's going on around her. But most of the time, she takes it in. And when she *does* decide to talk, it's always something worth waiting for.

Mrs. Barker sighed. "I don't think Trixie's owner, Jimmy Something-or-other, is too happy about Eddy's stepping in."

"Jimmy Green *Dinglehopper*," Catman said.

We drove through Loudonville to the fair-grounds and parked in the makeshift lot. The van doors slid open, and the Barker boys and their dogs scrambled out.

"We need to get these dogs to Barker!" Mr. Barker shouted, struggling to hold on to two-year-old William with one hand and Underdog's leash with the other. "Catman, Winnie, we'll see you inside!"

I climbed out Catman's door. A huge red-and-white-striped tent billowed in the distance. On the top waved a small yellow flag with *Circus* in white letters, as if anybody couldn't tell by the smell of peanuts and cotton candy and the sounds of organ-grinder music and throngs of laughing spectators.

"Funky, huh?" Catman whispered.

We weaved through crowds swarming the midway, past food stands on wheels, their lids propped up.

Catman cut over to a group of trailers. At the end of the row an elephant groaned, then flipped straw onto its back. Two men in gladiator costumes dashed by us. A muscular woman in a sequined bathing suit yelled at a man who would have made a tough Welsh Cob pony.

Catman walked straight to a group of lion cages on wheels. "Neat-o. These cats are happening."

Two of the lions stopped their growling and paw-swatting to stare at Catman.

I took a deep breath of lions and sawdust and . . . *horse!*

I peered past the cages, beyond the circus tent, to a long rectangular tent. I could just make out the sign: *Menagerie Tent.* A horse whinnied, and out of the tent stepped the most gorgeous black stallion I'd ever seen. His long, black mane flowed over a thick, arched neck. On his back sat a kid I guessed to be older than Catman. His wavy, black hair matched his stallion's. He was riding English-style in a red-and-gold uniform. He lifted his hat, and the powerful stallion tipped his nose to the ground in a grand bow.

"Catman . . . that horse . . ." My voice, which always sounds a little hoarse, came out a croak.

Suddenly the stallion bucked. His rider grabbed for the saddle and missed. The horse bucked again, and the boy flew off. The black stallion exploded into a gallop.

Someone screamed.

People scrambled out of the horse's path.

I stayed planted in the runway and watched

as the most powerful stallion I'd ever seen came barreling straight at me.

*W*innie!" I heard Catman shout, but I kept
my gaze on the racing stallion. Dust rose in
clouds. The thudding of hooves grew louder.

I was ready to dive out of the way if I had to.
But what I read in the black's eyes was fear.
"Easy, fella," I cooed, trying to make my voice
sound like a nicker.

I thought the stallion slowed a little. But still,
he kept coming.

I raised my arms out at my sides. He dropped
into a canter a few yards from me.

"Get out of the way!" someone shouted.

The stallion slid to a stop a foot in front of me.
He snorted and tossed his head, saying, *Are you
sure it's safe? I'm ready to get out of here if it's not.*

I inched toward him. He quivered. I blew into his nostrils, saying, *You can trust me.*

His nostrils flared in and out. Then he blew back, honoring me with a horse greeting.

I reached up and stroked his neck. From a distance I'd pegged him as an Andalusian, a regal Spanish breed. Now I could see he was probably a Morgan, the biggest, most powerful Morgan I'd ever seen.

"Man," Catman muttered, moving in beside me. He shook his head, and I could see that the normally cool Catman had beads of sweat on his forehead.

The tall, dark-haired rider came running up to us. "I can't believe Midnight did that! Thank you!" He did a double take of Catman. "Catman, who is this brave person?" He picked up his horse's reins.

"Winnie, Ramon," Catman said, pronouncing the name so it rhymed with *alone.*

Ramon shook my hand. "Ramon is my show name, but I prefer it to Raymond, my real name. And this bad boy is Midnight Mystery." He stroked the stallion's coal-black forehead. "Thanks again, Winnie."

Ramon had a muscled build and might have

been an Andalusian if he'd been a horse. "Are *you* okay?" I hated how gravelly my voice sounded.

"Sure." He turned to his horse. "I just don't know what's gotten into Midnight. I've always been able to count on him. Now, when it's more important than ever, he gets crazy on me."

"What's up, man?" Catman asked.

"You know my Russian cossack act?" Ramon asked. "Clyde Beatty Cole Brothers Circus, a *real* three-ring circus, is looking for a cossack act to tour with them next year. They're sending out a scout for our last performance. I've dreamed about working with them! And not just because they pay better and draw solid crowds." He laughed, showing perfect white teeth. Then the smile dissolved. "But it's not going to happen if Midnight keeps this up. My last two performances were terrible."

"You need Winnie," Catman said. "She fixes problem horses."

My cheeks felt on fire.

Ramon smiled at me. "I may have to take you up on that. I'd do anything to ride for that circus! My mom used to be their lead act."

"How old are you?" I couldn't believe I'd asked it out loud.

Note to self: Keep your big mouth shut!

"I mean, don't you go to school?" I asked.

Note to self: READ your notes to self.

But Ramon didn't look at me like I was the stupidest show on earth. "I'm 17, but thanks to the slave driver who homeschools me—" he grinned at Catman—"the honorable Colonel Coolidge, I'll finish high school in June. So I'd be free to travel with the Beatty Show." His eyes sparkled when he talked about his dream.

"Ramon!" a stern voice bellowed over all the other noise.

"Speak of the Colonel . . . thanks again, Winnie. See you later." Ramon left with Midnight, and Catman and I headed to the Big Top.

"Why doesn't Ramon's mother homeschool him?" I asked as we dodged a camel led by a woman in a red gown.

"She died," Catman explained.

I stopped walking. "What happened?"

Catman kept moving, so I had to scramble to catch him. "Circus accident."

Ramon's mother had starred in the big circus,

and now he wanted to star there too. I understood. "What about Ramon's dad?"

"Died before Ramon was born. Ramon lived with his grandmother, Florence, who had a high-wire act. After Great-Gran Coolidge died, the Colonel met Flo. They got married in the Moscow Circus."

I couldn't imagine what it would be like to lose *both* of my parents.

"When Flo left both of them, the Colonel unofficially adopted Ramon. Ramon was only 10, and they've traveled with the circus ever since."

We'd reached the back of the big circus tent. Catman nodded to a burly guy guarding the entrance, and we walked on in.

Spotlights shone on three dirt rings, but only the center ring looked busy. Two huge men moved pedestals around. A girl in a glittery swimsuit swung on a rope hanging from the top of the tent. From a high platform, a man pushed a swing, then grabbed it.

From the far side of the ring one of the clowns waved at us.

"Far out, Barker!" Catman shouted.

"Barker?" I squinted at the clown until I could

see Barker under the orange wig, painted face, and red clown nose.

We hurried across, dodging a tumbling clown, a juggler, and two beautiful white horses. Just as we got there, Barker's parents and brothers came running up, half of them munching cotton candy.

"You look great, Barker!" I punched the puffy sleeve of his green-striped clown costume. His tightly curled black hair peeked out from under the wig.

"Pray for me, Winnie!" Barker pleaded. "I haven't had much time to practice my act."

I liked that Barker wanted me to pray for him. He knew I had trouble talking to God, that I wasn't good at it like his family or my sister. So I shot up a quick prayer right then, thinking it was pretty cool to be able to talk to God anywhere, even at a circus.

Barker's brothers and their dogs crowded around him. I glanced at the exit and saw Ramon and Midnight just outside. I couldn't help feeling sad. Losing my mother had been the worst thing I could think of. But at least I wasn't an orphan like Ramon.

"You should be proud of your young joey here!"

I recognized the voice I'd heard outside yelling for Ramon. I turned to see a tall man in a red tuxedo and shiny black boots that came to his knees. His thick, gray hair had plenty of black left in it. The Colonel looked at home in his outfit, and it was easy to picture him leading men into battle in World War II.

"He's not *Joey!* He's Eddy!" Matthew snapped.

"A joey is another name for a clown, isn't it, Colonel?" Mrs. Barker asked.

"Intelligent as ever, madame!" said the Colonel. He turned to Mr. Barker's mother. "And how is the charming Granny Barker?" Colonel Coolidge bowed low, took her hand, and kissed it. She let him, and I think her eyes twinkled.

"Told you," Catman whispered. "He digs her." He raised his voice. "Colonel, Winnie. Winnie, Colonel Coolidge."

The Colonel clicked his heels together and did a stiff bow. It would have been hard to invent two people less alike than Catman and his great-grandfather. The Colonel was military-stiff, Catman rubbery. Where the Colonel was loud and blustery, Catman was soft and still. As a horse, the Colonel might have been a Maremmano, a classical Greek warhorse descended from sixteenth-century Spain. Catman was a Peruvian Paso, a smooth and steady breed with a weird gait kind of like swimming.

"I like your circus," I said, amazed at how dumb I could be talking to people. Give me horses any day.

"The circus is in my blood! I have the honor of being related to Colonel William Frederick Cody, known as Buffalo Bill, the world-famous Wild West hero. Calvin here might have followed in those footsteps."

I tried not to grin. Only Catman's parents, and I guess his great-grandfather, call him Calvin.

The Colonel tapped his perfectly polished boots with his ringmaster's whip. "Calvin's father, I am sad to say, never showed promise as a circus man. He lacked the discipline! Refused to polish his boots before bed."

"Winnie's a horse gentler," Catman announced.

The Colonel eyed me up and down. I felt my spine straighten, like I was under military inspection. "Do you live in Ashland?"

I nodded.

"Have you a horse?" he asked.

I nodded.

"Excellent!" the Colonel boomed. "Then you shall join our Ashland troupe and fill in as a greeter. Always a need for towners as greeters!"

A picture flashed into my mind—me, about seven or eight, screaming at Dad that I would run away and join the circus. "I don't think my dad would go for it." Part of me wanted to say yes. Nickers would be so great. But the last circus performance was the same night as Mom's birthday. "And we have plans for Friday. Thanks anyway, though."

"Think about it!" he roared. "Kings and queens have honored the circus with their presence! And on our last performance of the year, some of the greatest fighting men in history will be there looking on!"

Catman explained. "The Colonel's army buddies get together every five years for the last show of the season."

Colonel Coolidge bowed again. "My offer stands." Pivoting toward center ring, he bellowed, "Not there, you goober!" Under his breath, he muttered, "Roustabouts!"

When he stormed off, I felt my muscles relax again.

Catman and I sat with Granny, Mrs. Barker, Matthew, and William, while Mr. Barker, the other boys, and their dogs went with Barker.

I watched the greeters and imagined doing the same things with Nickers. A blonde girl about Ramon's age and someone who could have been her mother led beautiful white Lipizzaner horses around the ring, stopping to chat with groups in the bleachers or people straggling in.

"Gabrielle LeBlond and her mother," Catman said. "Horse acts."

The Colonel blew a whistle, and five minutes later he marched to the center ring and took off his top hat. "Ladies and gentlemen, welcome to Colonel Coolidge's Traveling Circus!"

Trumpets and trombones played circus music. Drums pounded as performers paraded around the rings. Gabrielle and her mom, dressed in white formals, rode their Lipizzaners sidesaddle. Behind them marched a short man cracking a long bullwhip. Then came a stream of clowns, trapeze artists, an elephant, a camel, and on and on.

"Catman!" A chubby clown hollered up. He tossed stilts into the bleachers.

I ducked, but Catman caught the stilts, leaped three rows down to the parade path, hopped onto the stilts, and joined the parade. Mrs. Barker and I cracked up as Catman stilted all the way around the circus tent, tossed back the stilts, and then took his seat as if nothing had happened.

The first circus act moved fast because the lion cages had been wheeled out as the parade cleared. Leopold, the short lion tamer, cracked his whip and opened the cages, turning his back on roaring lions as they stepped out.

Beside me, Catman adjusted his glasses and leaned forward.

All five lions mounted pedestals and sat up, batting the air as if clawing invisible enemies. But one lion was the star. At the end of the act, Leopold stuck his head in its jaws. The crowd gasped, then burst into applause.

Two men, who would have been Clydesdales in a horse world, lumbered out and rolled away the cages, while the chubby clown swept the ring.

"Ladies and gentlemen!" shouted Colonel Coolidge over the mike. "Our next act—!"

"Lookie! Eddy!" two-year-old William cried from Mrs. Barker's lap.

Barker, in clown costume, wandered into the ring, dragging Macho, Johnny's coon dog.

"Please clear the ring!" commanded the Colonel.

But Barker just waved as if he were happy to see the ringmaster.

Kids around us chuckled.

Barker and Macho ambled to the mike.

"The clown act isn't until later!" barked the ringmaster.

Barker stood on tiptoes to talk into the mike. "I'm not a clown. I'm a master trainer! I can teach a dog any trick!"

People laughed, including the Colonel. "Oh yes, you look like a master dog trainer!"

"I'll prove it!" Barker shouted. "I just found this stray dog, and I'll train him right now!"

Macho barked.

Mrs. Barker laughed hard.

Colonel Coolidge inspected the scroungy-looking hound dog. Then he sprang back, holding his nose, like Macho had bad breath. "Your dog's bark seems to be worse than his bite. Go ahead then. It's a *flea* country!" He muttered into the mike, "This circus is going to the dogs."

Barker turned to Macho. "Sit up!"

Macho obeyed.

"Lie down!" Barker commanded. "Roll over!"

Macho did. The crowd laughed and clapped.

"I don't believe you just found that dog!" the ringmaster accused.

From the side of the ring a chocolate Lab dressed in a baseball uniform trotted out to center stage—Mark's Irene.

Barker shouted, "Here's another stray!"

Irene sat on her haunches and didn't move while Barker rolled four straight balls past her.

"I thought you said you were a master dog trainer!" snapped the ringmaster. "Why did that dog just let four balls by?"

Barker shrugged. "Everybody knows you have to *walk* the dog!"

The drums hit a *ba-da-boom!* And the crowd roared with laughter.

William squealed as his collie trotted out with Luke's white Chihuahua on his back.

"Watch me teach these two strays some tricks!" Barker shouted.

But Colonel Coolidge held up his hand. "Wait just a minute! Any trick?"

Barker nodded and started to give the dogs a command.

The Colonel interrupted. "Let's have the audience decide which trick *they'd* like to see!"

Barker looked worried as the ringmaster invited the crowd to shout out tricks.

One by one, people shouted: "Play dead!" "Skip rope!" "Speak!"

A tall, skinny man with bushy, red hair stood up in front of us. He clutched popcorn in one hand, a laser flashlight in the other. "Make that little dog jump through your arms!"

The Colonel repeated the man's request.

"That's too hard!" I whispered to Catman.

Barker made a loop with his arms. Underdog, the collie, with Chico still on his back, ran toward Barker. As Underdog trotted past, Chico jumped through Barker's outstretched arms and landed back on Underdog.

The crowd went wild! Barker was a hit!

After that, we watched the trapeze and high-wire acts, the jugglers and acrobats. Catman answered my questions with as few words as humanly possible: "Double trapeze.

Roman rings. Cloud swing. Spanish web." He could have had his own man-of-few-words act.

Gabrielle and her mother did a great bareback act with two Percherons—big, gentle horses with calm dispositions, the kind that used to pull royal coaches or farm plows without complaining. Later the LeBlonds came out again—Gabrielle on her white horse, her mom on a camel, and her dad on an elephant. The elephant got the most applause.

I watched Gabrielle as they rode past. She had a big smile, but it looked fake. "She doesn't look happy," I told Catman.

"Gabrielle had the dancing-horse act with the Hoxie Brothers Circus until her family signed on with the Colonel," Catman explained. "She's weirded-out that Ramon gets top billing."

When Ramon and Midnight made their entrance, there was no doubt who was the star of the show. The crowd burst into applause as Midnight high-stepped to the center of the ring and bowed. Ramon took off his three-cornered hat as Midnight dropped to his knees, then lay down so Ramon could step off.

Midnight Mystery played dead, sat up, then stretched low for Ramon to mount again. But as soon as Ramon hit the saddle, Midnight changed. He sidestepped and jigged in place. Nothing too bad, but I knew it wasn't part of the show.

They moved to the outer ring, and Midnight did the two-step, marching with one leg, step, step, then reaching out the other leg, all to waltz music. I could hardly wait to see his cossack act, the one that could help him realize his dream.

"How about a big hand for Ramon and Midnight Mystery?" shouted the Colonel.

The crowd cheered as Midnight pranced to the center of the ring and lifted one hoof in a wave. They rode toward the exit. Then Midnight turned around and reared, both his forelegs pawing the air.

Suddenly Mystery lunged forward. Ramon slid in the saddle but stayed on. The stallion exploded into a dead canter, bolted around the ring and through the slit in the tent.

People applauded, but I knew better. "Catman! That was no act! Midnight Mystery is a runaway!"

$\mathcal{C}$atman passed me as we raced out of the Big Top after Ramon and Midnight. Behind us I heard the Colonel's ringmaster voice: "Ladies and gentlemen, another round of applause for Midnight Mystery's great getaway!"

The Colonel covered the runaway so smoothly, for a second I wondered if I'd imagined trouble. But I know a terrified horse when I see one.

I turned the corner to an open field and spotted Ramon sitting on the ground with Catman beside him.

"Not very impressive," Ramon said as I ran up to them. "Two spills in one day. I'm glad the circus scout wasn't around."

"That's a bad scene, man!" Catman helped Ramon up.

"I'll get your horse," I offered.

Ten yards away Midnight stood statue-still, his black skin twitching.

"Easy, boy," I coaxed. "We have to stop meeting like this."

Midnight let me walk up to him, but he jerked his head away. White circled his pupils, a sure sign of fear. Keeping my hands low, I scratched his chest, then moved slowly up his neck. Mom taught me that horses need scratching. If you can discover their favorite spots, they'll do almost anything for you. After a while, I found Midnight's soft spot under his wavy mane.

I led him back to Ramon. "Want me to cool him down?"

"Thanks, Winnie," Ramon said. "I hate that I missed my cossack act."

The Colonel's voice was announcing the return of the LeBlonds and their amazing Lipizzaners. They must have been covering for Ramon.

I unbuckled the silver-trimmed, brown saddle and slid it off with the blanket. Midnight side-stepped.

Catman and Ramon rushed to help me with the saddle.

"See how Midnight's back twitches?" I asked.

34

"Like it's sore or—ouch!" Something jabbed my hand as Catman took the saddle blanket from me.

I flipped the blanket over. A giant burr was stuck to the underside. "No wonder Midnight acted up!" I pulled out the burr. It looked like a miniature porcupine.

Ramon shook his head. "I check my equipment before every performance." He stroked Midnight's back. Midnight pranced in place, still unsettled. "I don't know what's wrong with him, but it's not just that burr." He turned to me. "Winnie, if you really can help horses, will you help Midnight Mystery? I have to get him back to normal before Friday!"

As I stared back at Ramon, I felt something horses sometimes experience. Two horses who want to break from a stable or get to greener grass can form an instant connection if they want the same thing. At that moment I knew Ramon and I wanted the same thing—to recapture a world that had included our mothers. I needed to put on a horse show just like my mom had. And Ramon needed to star in the circus that had once starred his mom. "I'll do everything I can," I promised.

The Barker children and dogs slept most of the drive back home. Catman and I thanked Mr. and Mrs. Barker and Granny Barker before hopping out at my house.

I was glad Catman got out with me, but I didn't envy him walking back to his place. The Coolidges live in a three-story mansion that could have starred as a haunted house in a horror movie. The first time I saw it, I thought the house was deserted.

We ran inside. "Dad! Lizzy!" I shouted. I couldn't wait to tell them about the circus.

Lizzy burst into the room in high-speed talking mode. With her dark hair and green eyes, my sister looks like I would if I were two inches taller, had better hair, and lost my freckles. Some people mistake us for twins, even though she's a year younger. "Winnie! Catman! You'll never believe this! It *so* rocks! Guess! No, you'd never guess!"

"Lizzy," I tried, "slow down."

"When they called, I answered. And they said, 'Didn't you get the confirmation packet?' And I said, 'Huh?' And they said, 'Oh no, you didn't get the tickets?' And I asked what they looked like and they told me. So I searched through that whole pile of mail Dad hasn't even touched, while they're still on the phone saying how they can't trust the mail anymore, but I found it! Straight from Chicago, with Dad's name on the envelope and—!"

"What are you talking about?" I interrupted.

"The Invention Convention, of course! Dad won the Inventor's Contest!"

"Far out!" Catman exclaimed.

"You're kidding!" I thought back to how Dad hadn't even wanted to enter the contest. Catman and I had talked him into it.

"Imagine!" Lizzy continued. "The Chicago Invention Convention! All expenses paid! I wish I could go with him. Remember Zack? Wasn't he in that school we went to in Chicago? One of the *I* states for sure. I'll bet by now he's—"

"Chicago?" I repeated. "Dad's going to Chicago? Flying?" Images of planes crashing and burning flashed to my brain. "On a plane?"

"Duh," Lizzy teased. "All the geese were booked."

I tore down the hall to Dad's bedroom.

"Winnie, you're back!" He pulled down an old suitcase from his closet.

Catman stepped in. "Groovy, Mr. W. Congrats!"

"Thanks, Catman." Dad plopped the suitcase onto his bed and dusted it with his sleeve. "I still can't believe I won! I have you two to thank. I never would have entered that contest if it hadn't been for you."

I didn't want any of that credit. What if the plane got hijacked? "Dad, don't go! I mean, you can't just leave Lizzy and me!"

Dad chuckled. "Don't worry, honey. Catman's parents have graciously offered to let you girls stay with them while I'm away. Bart's driving me to the airport Monday so I don't have to leave the cattle truck in the Cleveland parking garage. He offered to come pick up some of your things for the week."

"The week?" I repeated, a lot louder than Dad.

"I should be back sometime next Saturday night." He clicked the suitcase open.

"Dad, you can't go," I said quietly.

Dad frowned.

"Friday's Mom's birthday."

Dad's frown caved in deeper. He'd forgotten. I saw it in his eyes. My dad had forgotten Mom's birthday.

38

"I'm sorry, Winnie." His shoulders slumped. He was going to change his mind. I knew it. No way would my dad break Mom's birthday tradition.

Dad broke into a smile. "I know! We'll celebrate Sunday when I get back! How's that?"

"That stinks!" I shouted, feeling overheated, like the house's forced-air heater would suffocate me. "Mom's birthday isn't Sunday! It's Friday!"

Dad opened his dresser drawer and riffled through it. "Your mother would understand, Winnie. She always said I should take a chance and create. She said I could do anything. . . ."

I couldn't speak. My head pounded.

Lizzy walked in and plopped on the bed. "You are *so* lucky, Dad! Well, not luck. I mean, you must really be a great inventor! And Chicago! Sweet!"

"Lizzy, Dad wants to be gone on Friday!" Dad might be able to hold out against me, but not against Lizzy, who almost never argues with him. "We have to watch *Lady and the Tramp*, and—" I didn't want to give away the horse show surprise—"and eat spaghetti!"

"Hey!" Lizzy cried, sitting up cross-legged.

"We can do it when Dad gets back! I've got Power of the Pen on Friday anyway. You know, that essay competition in Mansfield?"

Was I the only one who cared? Tears pushed at my eyes, making my head throb harder.

Dad put his hands on my shoulders. "Winnie, I'm sorry about all this. Although I have to admit, I thought you'd be happy for me."

I shook him off. I *wasn't* happy for him. I wasn't happy for me or anybody else.

"Hey! There's no school on Friday. Teacher's convention, I think. Maybe you and Catman can do something fun together!" Lizzy suggested.

I didn't want fun. I wanted Mom. And if I couldn't have her, couldn't I at least have her birthday? What was wrong with them? Had they changed so much they didn't even miss Mom?

"Fine!" I snapped. I didn't need them. I'd celebrate Mom's birthday on my own. They could have their lives, and I'd have mine. Colonel Coolidge had invited Nickers and me to be greeters, and greeters we'd be! "You and Lizzy can do whatever you want! *I'm* joining the circus!"

$\mathcal{I}$ cried myself to sleep that night after a picture of every one of Mom's birthday horse shows had flashed through my brain.

It wasn't until the middle of the night that Dad's words sank in. I bolted straight up in bed, sheets tangled around me. Lizzy and I were moving into Coolidge Castle!

Sunday morning I walked through cold dawn darkness to the barn. I needed a bareback ride on Nickers to clear my head. Early frost clung to fallen leaves, turning the pasture into a giant bowl of frosted cereal flakes.

When I finished riding Nickers, I took a spin on Hawk's Appaloosa. Towaco had started out in the ritzy Stable-Mart, owned by Spider Spidell, who seems to have multiple arms clutching his Ashland businesses: A-Mart Department Store, Pet-Mart, Pizza-Mart, Burger-Mart, and Stable-Mart. Towaco, like all horses in Spidells' sterile, unfriendly stable, had been caged in his stall nearly 24 hours a day. No wonder he'd turned into a problem horse.

Mr. Spidell's daughter, Summer, and I tried to stay out of each other's way, which wasn't easy since we had some of the same classes in middle school. To Summer Spidell and her friends, I'd never be Winnie the Horse Gentler. I was nothing more than Odd-Job Willis's kid, a wild Mustang to Summer's classy American Saddle Horse.

By the time I'd finished brushing, mucking, and feeding, I had to head in to get ready for church. Maybe by now Dad had come to his senses. I imagined him downing a giant Lizzy-breakfast and waiting to tell me he'd changed his mind about Chicago.

But nobody was in the kitchen. Not even the reliable scent of Sunday pancakes was there.

Instead, I heard Dad and Lizzy laughing as they searched for jokes Dad could use in his acceptance speech. He wasn't even going to church with us. In Wyoming, Mom had seen to it that we never missed church. Although Dad had stopped going after Mom died, since we'd moved to Ashland, he'd started up again.

But not this Sunday. He had to get ready for Chicago.

Catman showed up late for church and sat by me in the Barker pew. I asked him to tell his great-grandfather that Winnie Willis and Nickers were signing on as circus greeters for Ashland.

After church, I didn't feel like talking to Dad. I changed clothes and tried to leave before he could say another word about Chicago.

I'd made it to the front door when Dad caught me. "Winnie! There you are! You slipped out this morning before we could talk." He was wearing an orange jumpsuit, and he hadn't shaved. I guess people think my dad's handsome, but right then he looked more like a prisoner than an inventor. "So . . . the circus . . . the Invention Convention . . . we're okay?"

My dad isn't much better at communicating than I am.

"I'm in a rush, Dad." I jerked the door open and hurried out.

"Winnie?" Dad's voice faded as I closed the door and ran down the steps.

I didn't stop running until I reached the brick building where I work part-time for Pat Haven. I stopped to catch my breath and stared at the picture window, where faded white letters spelled out *Pat's Pets*.

Pat's round face appeared through the glass. She waved, then came around to open the door. Pat's not only my boss. She's the substitute teacher for my life science class *and* our land-lord. She's also my friend. Pat's not much taller than me. When she laughs, her brown curls bounce across her forehead. My mom would have called her "spirited." They would have liked each other.

I stepped inside and let the warmth of the pet shop soak in.

"You must be proud as a peacock of your daddy!" Pat tapped the birdcage. "No offense!" She never fails to apologize to animals for her animal expressions.

The weird thing was that I *was* proud of Dad. I just didn't want him to go. "Did you know he has to fly to Chicago, Pat?"

"Lizzy told me. Isn't that something!"

"It's not safe! And what if he likes Chicago so much he wants to stay?" I swallowed the lump that popped into my throat whenever I thought about Dad leaving. "I just wish he'd stay home."

"If wishes were fishes . . . ," Pat started. She glanced at the aquarium. "No offense." She squeezed my shoulder. "Let him go, sugar. He'll be back."

But Pat didn't know that. Nobody did.

Pat walked upstairs to her little apartment while I booted up the computer and logged onto the Pet Help Line. Barker had created the homepage. He handles all dog questions, Catman the cat questions. And if anyone asks about birds, we ask Hawk. Her real name is Victoria Hawkins. She's good with her horse, Towaco, but her real love is birds. I'm in charge of horse mail. I only had one new e-mail since Saturday:

> Dear Winnie the Horse Gentler,
> My horse, Peanut, is so stubborn!

I bought her from a farm down the road, where she was foaled. Now, whenever she can, Peanut runs back 2 her old barn! What's wrong with her?
—Newgraymare

As I answered the e-mail, I felt like crying for Peanut.

Dear Newgraymare,
    Nothing is wrong with your horse! Try to understand her. She wants her old home, her mother's barn. Why wouldn't she?! Since Peanut can't live there anymore, you should try to make her new home as much like her old barn as possible. Maybe that will help.
—Winnie the Horse Gentler

Pat bustled by. "I'm off! Got to get these puppies to the Loudonville Nursing Home. Those folks *love* newborns!"

"Loudonville?" I asked, logging off the help line. "Pat, could you give me a lift to the circus?" I knew if I got there, Barkers would bring me home. "I promised Ramon I'd try to help Midnight Mystery." And unlike some, *I* wouldn't break my promise. True, Lizzy and Dad may not have promised in so many words how we'd always celebrate Mom's birthday. But an unspoken promise can be every bit as strong as a spoken one.

The puppies yapped all the way to Loudonville. After Pat dropped me off, I roamed the circus grounds. Performers in regular clothes bounced on a trampoline. Men carried ropes and poles into the Big Top. An elephant lumbered by, his trainer struggling to keep at his hip.

"Winnie!" Ramon ran up. "You came!"

Ramon walked me to the menagerie tent. I felt as awkward as a wild Mustang. But as soon as I saw Midnight, I relaxed. Horses I could handle. Inside the tent, an elephant lifted a trunkload of hay to his mouth. The chain around one back leg didn't look like it could hold him if he'd wanted to leave. A group of white horses took up the other end of the tent, with llamas, a camel, and a few empty stalls between.

"It's great you're going to be an Ashland greeter," Ramon said as he untied his stallion.

We led the Morgan to a field behind the tent, and for 20 minutes I just played with him. I could already feel myself getting attached. Mom used to call it an occupational hazard. Midnight nuzzled my neck, followed me, and let me ride him without a saddle.

I slid off his broad back and nodded to Ramon. "Your turn."

"Bareback?"

"Bareback," I answered. "The last thing you need is that big saddle between you and your horse. I want you to *feel* him."

Ramon swung onto Midnight's back with ease. "So how do I stop him from bolting?"

I patted Midnight's shoulder. "First, don't ever punish Midnight for bolting."

"How's he going to know it's wrong?" Ramon protested.

"It's not *wrong!*" I insisted. "Flight is how horses survive. When he's ready to bolt, speak to him in his own language."

I showed Ramon where Midnight liked to be scratched, and he leaned forward to reach under Midnight's mane. "I can feel him relax all right." Ramon sat back up. "Still, that's not going to stop him from bolting like he did last night."

"You can't stop a true bolt," I admitted. "Horses are too powerful. But if you can sense trouble *before* it happens, you can redirect the power. Feel for his heart, for stiffness through his back. Sense tension in the reins."

"And if I miss it and he bolts?"

"Get him to do this." I led Midnight in a tiny circle. "Use short, give-and-take tugs to get him to flex his neck and lower his nose. If you can control his nose, the rest of him will follow."

We practiced for an hour, and Ramon and Midnight got better at reading each other.

"You got it!" I called. "Get him to drop his head. That will slow his heart rate. Then reward him with a scratch."

Ramon slid off Midnight's rump. *"I'm* the one who needs a reward! This is hard work! Maybe I should switch to a car."

"It's the same! You still have to tap the brakes in a skid. Cars are impossible to stop. . . ." A photo of my mom's accident flashed in my brain—the car losing control on the ice, the snowbank rushing up at us.

"Winnie, are you okay?" Ramon asked.

I tried to smile, but the accident photos wouldn't stay down. People think having a photographic memory is some kind of super gift. It might be . . . if I got to choose the photos. But I don't.

Ramon bent down to peer into my face. "Can I help?"

Part of me wanted to tell him about Mom. He might have understood. He'd lost both of his parents. But I couldn't do it.

"You've been great helping me," Ramon insisted. "Sure there isn't something I could do for you?"

I started to say no. Then I thought of something. "Ramon, I need to know how to teach a horse to bow."

Ramon showed me exactly how he'd trained Midnight to bow. I watched, then tried it myself, picking up tips for Nickers. No matter where Lizzy and Dad might be on Mom's birthday, I was still putting on the horse show for my mom.

Colonel Coolidge shouted from his trailer. "Ramon! Your history report!"

"I better go. He's so edgy, getting ready for his war buddies. I think they're down to four left now."

"Are they all coming?" I asked.

50

Ramon shrugged. "They don't write or talk to each other for five years, but they always show up wherever we are for the last performance."

"How do they know where to find the Colonel?"

Ramon laughed. "They were an intelligence unit! Spies."

"Ramon!" bellowed Colonel Coolidge.

"I'll put Midnight away," I offered.

"Thanks. The Colonel waits for no man! Later!" Ramon ran toward the Colonel's trailer.

I walked Midnight back to the menagerie tent, which was becoming my favorite place at the circus, filled with overpowering smells of elephant, camel, and horse. At the end of the row Gabrielle LeBlond was making her horse bow, just like Midnight.

I strolled up to her. "Your horse is fantastic!"

She glanced at me, then turned back to her horse and made a quick hand motion. The Lipizzaner buckled down, leaned over, and rolled flat on his side.

"Wow! I'm Winnie. I know you're Gabrielle. Probably not your real name, right?"

"I *am* Gabrielle LeBlond," she said, so coldly I pictured frost around the words. She'd pulled her blonde hair up off her neck with a silver barrette. Her pale skin and barely blue eyes reminded me of Summer Spidell.

"Um . . . must be fun . . . riding your horse there and all." *Could I sound any dumber?*

"Do you mind? I'm trying to work here." She gave me a sneer that made me feel like a horse-fly.

Note to self: Ask Summer Spidell if she has a twin.

$\mathcal{I}$ walked the circus midway until I bumped into Mr. Barker and Mark, who told me where to find Catman. Circling back, I headed for the lion cages, where Catman was silently communing with the kings of beasts.

"I dig these cool cats," he whispered, not taking his gaze off them.

"There you are!" A red-haired clown in a battered straw hat and a green-striped costume strode toward us with legs so long his flappy clown shoes didn't look out of place. White paint covered his face, and his eyes were large, black triangles. But even the painted, red clown smile couldn't disguise his frown. "I want you to juggle!"

"Not tonight." Catman hadn't stopped staring down the lions.

"Juggle?" I asked.

"Who's she?" The clown spit out the question.

Without turning around, Catman introduced us. "Winnie Willis, Jimmy Green Dinglehopper."

"You're the clown Barker's replacing, right?" I asked.

"Wrong!" he snapped. "Nobody replaces Jimmy Green!" He turned to Catman, who had crouched to the lions' eye level. "There's too much dog act now. You could break it up, share the slot, juggle like you did last year."

Catman was a juggler?

Catman shook his head, unmoved.

Swearing, the angry clown stormed off. I had to dodge out of his way.

Catman wouldn't leave the lions until their tamer came for them.

"Cool cats!" Catman commented, as three other men arrived to wheel the cages into the Big Top.

Leopold, the lion tamer, nodded, his face blank. His stubby beard looked like Dad's when Dad forgets to shave. He reminded me of a Shetland pony—small but tough.

"Catman loves your lions!" I said, trying to make conversation, which I should never do because I'm lousy at it.

Leopold glanced at me, then helped roll one of the lion cages away.

"Nice meeting you too," I muttered.

"He doesn't talk," Catman explained.

I felt awful. "Sorry! I didn't know." *Open mouth, insert foot!*

Note to feet: Stop jumping to conclusions and ending up in my mouth.

We found Mrs. Barker, Matthew, and William in the stands. This time I studied the greeters— how Barker used Chico the Chihuahua to welcome families as they walked in, the way the LeBlond Lipizzaners did tricks for groups of spectators. Jimmy Green Dinglehopper made people laugh by balancing a bowling pin on his nose or walking on his hands.

I imagined Nickers and me in the ring, bowing to the crowds.

"I wanna light!" William cried, pointing to a guy selling laser flashlights and coloring books.

"I told you, William. If I get you the light, you can't get candy later." Mrs. Barker was as patient with her kids as Mom had been with her horses.

"Light!" William screamed. "I want light!"

How did Lizzy babysit all five little Barkers at once?

"Well, look who's come to the circus!" Matthew Barker exclaimed.

Mrs. Barker waved as the whole Spidell family walked in. Summer and her older brother, Richard, stepped cautiously, as if they were afraid of sawdust. They took seats closest to the exit.

Barker bounded over to them, and he and Chico ran through their greeting routine. I'm good at telling a laugh *at* from a laugh *with*. The Spidells laughed *at* Barker.

The show went on, but the Spidells left before the second act.

When Midnight Mystery galloped out, I stood up and applauded. The tricks went well. Midnight seemed skittish, but nothing that would keep Ramon from doing his cossack act. I couldn't wait.

"And now," shouted the ringmaster, a.k.a. Colonel Coolidge, "we will give our performers a short break while we take a brief intermission!"

Shouts rang out for "Popcorn!" "Peanuts!" "Cotton candy!"

"I want that!" William screamed as a girl flashed a laser light at us in a strong, white beam.

Mrs. Barker kept calm. "I don't think we'll buy anything until you can ask nicely, William."

After a while the Colonel strode to center ring. "Ladies and gentlemen! Welcome back to Colonel Coolidge's Traveling Circus!"

A tall man sat in front of me. I had to peer around his bushy red hair to see.

Red hair! It was the same guy who'd sat in front of us the night before! And again he was loaded down with popcorn in one hand and a laser light in the other.

The audience loved Barker's act. Colonel Coolidge added a couple of joking asides to the crowd, like "This dog is so lazy, he only chases parked cars!"

It was the first resemblance I'd seen between Catman's great-granddad and his dad. Bart Coolidge owns Smart Bart's Used Cars, and he has a million stupid car jokes.

When the ringmaster asked the audience to name tricks for Barker's "strays," several people hollered out. But again the red-haired guy in front of us shouted the loudest: "Jump through your arms!"

"Catman," I whispered, "something's not right about that guy. I just can't put my finger on it. . . ."

Then I got it. "He's a clown!" I shouted, pointing at the red head of Jimmy Green Dinglehopper.

"Is he?" Mrs. Barker asked. "Oh, I see."

Matthew reached up and pulled the man's hair. "Where's the rest of your clown costume?" he demanded.

Dinglehopper snarled over his shoulder. "Don't bug me, kid!"

Down in the ring, Chico jumped through Barker's arms, and the crowd cheered. If Jimmy Green wanted to wreck Barker's act, he wasn't doing a very good job of it.

The rest of the show went smoothly, and finally, the moment I'd waited for arrived.

"And now . . . ," bellowed the ringmaster, ". . . the Russian Cossack, Ramon, and his magnificent Midnight Mystery!"

When the music blared, Ramon and Midnight charged the arena. They could have been a vision—the powerful, black stallion in a flat saddle and silver armor, Ramon in a gray Russian soldier's uniform, with high black boots and fur cap. The Clyde Beatty Cole Brothers Circus would be crazy not to sign them up on the spot.

While Midnight galloped around the ring, Ramon vaulted off and on his horse, then swung to the side, seeming to hold on with one arm. The crowd gasped as he dangled off Midnight's rump, stood on his back, and slid under his belly.

In that instant, I saw a flash cross Midnight's face. The horse sprang from the ground as if he'd been bitten by a rattlesnake. Ramon scrambled back into the saddle as Midnight's hooves pawed the air. The stallion reared so high, so long, I was sure he'd fall over backwards, crushing Ramon.

Help them! I prayed, wishing I had words like Lizzy's. She'd have known exactly what to say.

Then I saw Ramon reach one hand to Midnight's neck and stroke him under the mane.

Yes! Calm him. Get him down!

Midnight's hooves dropped to the ground. Ramon lowered the stallion's head, and Midnight burst into a canter. Ramon made him circle, controlling the power. He'd done it!

"Let's have a big round of applause for

Ramon and Midnight Mystery!" shouted the Colonel.

The crowd applauded, but I think even they knew the stallion's behavior hadn't been part of the act.

"There!" William shouted. *"That* light! I want one like that man has!" He squirmed off his mother's lap and wriggled next to Dinglehopper's laser light.

I tried to remember the instant before Midnight reared. I'd seen a flash! A laser beam!

"You!" I cried, jumping to my feet and grabbing the laser light out of Jimmy Green Dinglehopper's hand. *"You* scared Midnight on purpose!"

$\mathcal{M}$y heart pounded like a herd of stamped-ing Mustangs as I stared from the laser light back to Jimmy Green Dinglehopper's bright red hair. "How could you!" I ached for Midnight, feeling his terror.

Catman stepped beside me. "Chill, Winnie." He slipped the flashlight out of my hand and gave it back to Dinglehopper. "Sorry, man."

"What—?" I started.

But Catman was forcefully guiding me down the bleachers and outside the tent.

"Catman! You don't understand! I saw a light flash in Midnight's eyes right before he reared! Your clown had a laser light!"

"So did lots of cats."

"Listen to me, Catman!" I felt like a detective

trying to wrap my brain around the clues. "Remember how Dinglehopper shouted out the hardest tricks for Barker's dogs?"

Catman raised his eyebrows at me. "Part of the act, Winnie."

That was part of the act? I thought about it. Of course it was! I felt like an idiot.

I tried to cover. "Well . . . sure . . . of course. But you have to admit he doesn't want the circus to look good when he's not star clown! Remember how he tried to get you to share Barker's spot? Even Mrs. Barker said he wasn't happy about Barker taking over. I think he shined that light in Midnight's eyes on purpose. I don't know why he's picking on Ramon's act, but—"

"I'm on it," Catman announced quietly.

I frowned up at him. "You're on it?" Did Catman think *he* was a detective now? I took a deep breath to keep from exploding. "Look . . . Dinglehopper had the flashlight." I thought about last night. *"And* Dinglehopper could have put that burr under Midnight's saddle!"

"Or not," Catman said simply.

Note to self: Catman Coolidge can be the most frustrating human on earth. And that's saying something.

By the time we left the circus, the wind had kicked up, along with a drizzling rain, and slapped wet leaves against the Barker bus windshield.

I thanked the Barkers for the ride and got out alone in front of my house. A pale light glowed from the front window. I dreaded going in and seeing Dad happily getting his inventions ready for his trip. I didn't know what to say to him.

When Mom died, neither of us had known what to say to each other. Lizzy had carried all three-way conversations while Dad and I tried to stay out of each other's way. Things had been getting so much better since we'd settled in Ashland. But now it felt like Dad and I had been thrown backward into the silence.

Instead of running to the house, I headed for the one place I always felt safe. With Nickers. Before I reached the barn, my horse nickered, a low rumbling that rattled my heart.

"Hey, girl." I wrapped my arms around her neck. Just breathing the same air as Nickers helped. I closed my eyes and listened to the music of rain drumming the roof, bare branches scratching the windows, Towaco shuffling in his

63

stall, and Nelson, my barn cat, purring from Nickers' hay trough.

Finally I dashed back across the junky yard, dodging raindrops, to my front door. I found Lizzy at the kitchen table, practicing for Power of the Pen, and Dad giving his acceptance speech to the mirror in his bedroom.

After a hot bath, I hollered good night and climbed into bed. Usually I can see the pasture through my bedroom window, but not tonight. Not even a trace of moonlight broke through the dark.

Monday morning Lizzy and I got up early to throw clothes into laundry sacks for Mr. Coolidge to pick up and haul to the haunted castle. I could hear Dad grunting from the living room as he tried to fit a backward bike into a cardboard box.

"I don't know what's so great about the back bike. How could it win an invention contest?" I muttered. The bike goes frontward like a regular bike, but you have to pedal backward. Big deal.

Barking sounded from the living room. "It's

just the new bike horn!" Dad shouted. "Think Barker will like it?" The bike he'd be showing off in Chicago really belonged to Barker, or it would on Christmas. Barker's parents were buying it for him. Dad barked the horn again.

"Barker will love it, Dad!" Lizzy shouted back.

Catman's bike meowed or sounded like a tornado. I never used my horn, so I had no idea how Dad had rigged it.

Dad dragged the long bike box back to show us. "I made a handle," he said, carrying the thing by what looked like the top of a picture frame.

Maybe airport security wouldn't let Dad on with a contraption like that. Maybe they'd send him back home where he belonged.

Dad was so excited I don't think he even noticed that I was giving him the silent treatment.

Lizzy made up for it. "Don't worry about anything, Dad! We'll be fine . . . although I wish you'd talked to Mrs. Barker before you signed us up at the Coolidges." She shuddered. "But we'll be just fine! Or even Pat might have let us stay with her—although I guess she wouldn't have room for us. Oh! And don't forget to look up Zack when you get to Chicago! I sat next to him in—"

I escaped to the barn, where I fed Towaco and Nickers. As soon as Nickers finished her grain, I led her to the paddock. I had a half hour before school. "Let's try that bow, girl."

I used every trick Ramon had shown me—pressure to the halter, holding a handful of oats where I wanted her to lower her head, tickling in a different spot. But nothing worked. Nickers had no desire to bow. Maybe it just wasn't my day.

"Winnie!" Lizzy's shout reached the paddock.

I kissed Nickers good-bye and walked to the yard, but I didn't see my sister until she dropped from the branches of an oak tree. She had a lizard in each hand—Larry, her fence lizard, and one I didn't recognize. Lizzy had built two homes for her lizard menagerie—one in a tree, and one underground.

"Go tell Dad good-bye!" she commanded.

I trudged inside and found Dad straightening his skinny black tie in the hall mirror. "How do I look, Winnie?"

"Okay." I gazed at his image in the mirror as if he were a stranger. Tall, dark, probably even handsome, for a parent. I wanted to beg him to please, please not go. To tell him I'd do anything if he just wouldn't get on that airplane, if he wouldn't leave, if he'd stay for Mom's birthday.

But it wouldn't have done any good. "Bye, Dad."

Dad turned and hugged me awkwardly.

I let him.

Then I biked to school.

Barker rode up as I was jiggling my bike into the rack. "Winnie!" Barker has the best smile, but even it couldn't get me to smile back. "How's Nickers? You're going to love being a circus greeter!"

"Ramon's helping me with the bow." I waited for Barker while he did his bike lock. I didn't have one. People don't steal backward bikes.

"The Colonel said my brothers could be butchers in the Ashland Circus. That's what they call people who sell junk at intermission. Maybe Lizzy would like to do it too."

As usual, a group of the popular kids stood outside, blocking the middle school entrance. Students and their cliques aren't that different from the Mustang herds Mom and I got to observe one summer. Horses in one herd stick together, almost never letting a strange horse in.

Summer Spidell reigned as queen of the popular "herd" at our school. I glanced at her, flanked by the two most popular boys in school, Grant and Brian. Summer wore designer jeans that looked as different from my jeans as a formal from a nightgown. Grant Baines was okay for a popular kid. I'd worked with his problem Quarter Horse.

Salena, a.k.a. Sal, waved at me with no-finger black gloves. Her red hair had a black streak in it, and I could see her fake lashes from yards away. She's okay though.

Hawk—Victoria Hawkins to her popular friends—came down the steps to meet Barker and me. Before I helped her with her horse, Towaco, Hawk used to act like she didn't know me at school. We have a funny relationship, but I think of her as a friend.

"I hear you are in the circus, Barker." Hawk wore leather pants and a matching jacket, black like her long, straight hair. I'm not sure what percentage American Indian she is.

"You should sign on as a greeter, like Winnie did." Barker turned to me.

I felt bad. I should have called Hawk about the circus. But I hate the phone. It's hard enough to talk to people when you can see their reactions. "We'll get Catman to ask the Colonel," I said. "You and Towaco would be great! We could have fun, Hawk."

She glanced over her shoulder at her friends. "Maybe not."

We were quiet for a minute.

"Victoria!" Summer shouted from the steps. "You have to hear this!"

"See you," Hawk said, trotting back to her herd.

I started up the steps, with Barker behind me.

"Why would he wear that ridiculous costume?" Summer was saying between giggles. "Besides, have you ever heard of an African-American clown? I didn't think they liked to paint their faces."

I shouldn't have been surprised. Summer has rotten things to say to and about everybody. But this felt worse, maybe because of the race slam, or maybe because Barker never had a rotten thing to say about anybody, not even Summer. I hurried inside, hoping Barker would hurry too, and that he hadn't heard what Summer had said. If Barker hadn't been there, I might have gone straight over and gotten in Summer's face. *Didn't think* they *liked to paint their faces?* I felt like painting *her* face.

Barker went ahead to class, but I made a side trip to the bathroom. While I was in a stall, I heard Summer walk in with Sal. I could pick her voice out of a lineup of the world's snottiest females.

"Tell me the truth, Sal," Summer whined. "Do I look fat in these jeans?"

Summer Spidell couldn't have looked fat if she'd wanted to.

"Those jeans are tight!" Sal exclaimed. "As in, they rock, Summer!"

They must have been standing by the mirrors, only a few feet away from my stall.

"I still can't get over it!" Summer sniveled. "Is it even possible to gain three pounds in two weeks? Maybe there's something wrong with me."

Talk about the understatement of all time!

"Has anybody said anything to you?" Summer insisted. "It's my stupid grandmother's fault. She baked cakes and cookies."

Sal laughed. "You can't even notice, Summer!"

I heard the bathroom door open and Summer mutter as they left, "I hope you're right."

I hustled to English and slid in next to Barker. If our teacher, Ms. Brumby, said anything noteworthy during class, I didn't note it. All I could think about was Dad. I imagined him in the car on the way to the airport, at the ticket counter, at the gate. In my next two classes I pictured Dad flying through gray clouds on his way to Chicago.

My last class before lunch was life science. Pat Haven had been our substitute teacher since the first day of class. I hoped the regular teacher never came back from wherever he went to "find himself," as our principal had told us.

Pat leaned on her desk. She looked like a cowgirl in her denim skirt and red-checked shirt. "Guess what! I'm about to give you the best assignment you ever got!"

Groans broke out at the word *assignment*.

Pat grinned. "You're going to the circus!"

Summer objected. "No way!"

"You'll each write a report on a circus animal," Pat continued. "Colonel Coolidge's circus is one of the few that treat animals with respect. Why, he rescued most of those critters from other circuses or zoos. Plus, he's graciously giving us promo tickets! So you get in free Thursday or Friday, when the show moves to Ashland!"

"Cool!" exclaimed Kaylee, a pretty girl who looked like she'd been born in China, but spoke better English than I did.

"Sounds good to me," Grant said.

"No it doesn't!" Summer griped. "Not if it's the same Podunk circus I saw in Loudonville."

Catman's great-grandfather's circus was *not* Podunk. I glanced over at Barker. He was staring at his desk, and I *knew* he'd heard Summer on the steps. I couldn't stand that she'd gotten to him. Eddy Barker is about the nicest person I've ever met.

I should have said something. I should have stood up for Barker, for Catman, for the circus. I opened my mouth and could feel my throat close off, daring me to try to get words out. So I didn't even try.

At lunch, Barker didn't talk much more than Catman. M joined us. I don't know what *M*

stands for. He's in my English class, always wears black, and rarely speaks, except for the time he blew everybody away in a class debate we had on abortion. Most of the time he makes Catman look talkative.

"Barker?" I asked while he and I ate our sandwiches and Catman and M gobbled cafeteria macaroni with barbeque on day-old buns. "What do you think of Jimmy Green Dinglehopper?"

"He's something," Barker admitted. "He's thrown me a couple of curves from the bleachers. I told him I wasn't sure Chico was ready for the jumping trick. But it worked out."

I gave Catman an I-told-you-so look.

"Hey, Barker!" Summer Spidell leaned back from her table right behind ours. "Are you going to be a clown in the Ashland circus?" She sounded like she might break into laughter any second.

Barker wadded up his lunch bag. Then he got his smile back. "Yeah, I am, Summer."

"A real circus clown—right here in our own cafeteria!" Summer exclaimed, grinning at Brian next to her. "Winnie, are you joining the circus too?"

I'd have bet money she already knew the

answer. I scooted closer to her and said as
sweetly as if I'd been Lizzy and meant it, "Yes
I am. Thanks for asking! Oh, and Summer, the
circus asked me to talk to you. They'd like you
to think about joining up."

In spite of herself, a smug, self-satisfied look
crossed Summer's face. "The circus wants *me?*"

"Yep, *you!* Colonel Coolidge says what the
Ashland circus really, really needs is—" I leaned
in closer, so only Summer could hear—"a fat
lady!"

The last sound I heard as I exited the cafeteria
was Summer's shrill gasp. It felt good to see
Summer Spidell finally swallow a dose of her
own medicine . . . even if I knew I'd feel a little
guilty later.

$\mathcal{H}$awk was already at Pat's Pets when I got there after school. Her Indonesian parrot, a red chattering lory with bright green-and-yellow wings, actually left her shoulder and flew to me.

"Hey, Peter!" I cooed. Hawk had named him Peter Lory after an actor she liked to watch in old scary movies.

"Hey!" Peter squawked. *"Peter good bird!"* He deserted me for Hawk when she walked up.

"Winnie, I believe it is wonderful that you and Nickers will perform in Ashland's circus." Hawk could teach English to the English. She pronounces each word razor sharp.

"Do you, Hawk?" I wish she'd said so in class or the cafeteria today.

She nodded. "Come, Peter! Good-bye, Winnie."

75

Hawk left, and I read over Barker's shoulder as he answered the dog e-mails on the Pet Help Line. He was on his last question:

Dear Barker,
    I love my German shepherd, Togo, but he plays too rough! He knocks me down if I don't open the door or set down his food dish fast enough. He's too bossy! What can I do?
—Dave the dog lover

Barker bit his bottom lip, then typed:

Dear dog lover,
    You need to think like a dog! Declare yourself leader of the pack. Sounds like Togo has the role now. Don't be bossy though. Just take control. Refuse to give him everything he wants when he wants it. Make him sit before you let him outside. When he does, pet him and let him out. Same with the food. He'll be happier, and so will you!
—Barker

Barker swiveled around and grinned at me. "Want to see Catman's latest advice?"

"You bet!" I loved reading what Catman wrote to people about their cats.

Oh, Catman!
My cat, Priscilla, loves everybody . . . except my boyfriend, Tray. Tray really tries, too. He calls my kitty, picks her up, everything. I thought maybe Priscilla knew something I didn't, so I broke up with Tray. Now he won't even speak to me. Help!
—Miss Kitty

Catman had written:

Like, chill, Miss Kitty!
Your boyfriend blew it by trying too hard with Pris. If he played hard-to-get, ignoring your kitty, Pris would come right to him. If you want Tray back, follow Pris's lead. Ignore him. On the other paw, Pris may be hip to something we don't know about Tray. I'd stick with Pris. Cats don't borrow money from you or drive too fast.
—Catman

Before I tackled the horse e-mails, I ran a computer search on Jimmy Green Dingle-hopper. I tried all possible names, from Jimmy Green to James Dinglehopper. I used five search engines and came up with the same answer: no such person.

That clown was not who or what he claimed to be. I raced through my e-mails, saving the most interesting for last:

Dear Winnie the Horse Gentler,
I take the best care of my horse! I buy her the most expensive saddles, bridles, and halters. I even put Margaret on the same expensive feed my uncle gives his racehorses. And how does my mare thank me? By acting fussy and high-strung (and she's not!). Even sunlight spooks my horse now!
—High-strung Harriet

I knew right away what the problem was:

Dear Harriet,
Stop feeding racehorse food to your horse! It's high-energy and guaranteed to make any horse nervous. Use regular

grain. Add a little oil to calm her until
she's back to normal.
—Winnie the Horse Gentler

I'd started biking home when Catman whis-
tled from his bike. I turned to see him pointing
in the direction of *his* home. My home, too,
now. I turned around and followed him.

"No lawn ornaments?" I asked as we wheeled
our bikes through the tall, dead grass of the
Coolidge yard. The only thing Mr. Coolidge
mowed was a strip in front of the porch, used
year-round for plastic lawn ornaments. Normally
Halloween pumpkins would stay out until the
Thanksgiving turkeys went up.

"The Colonel hates lawn ornaments," Catman
explained.

We parked our bikes on the porch and
walked in.

I'll never get used to the difference between
the inside and the outside of Coolidge Castle.
Outside, all three stories needed painting. A
couple of windows had boards nailed across
them in *X*s. Inside, polished staircases wound
from wood floors to high ceilings of shiny rafters
and glittering chandeliers. The red velvet furni-

ture could have been in a fancy museum, showing how rich people lived a hundred years ago.

Mrs. Coolidge came swooping down the stairs in a lime-green bathrobe and matching fuzzy slippers. Her hair was in pin curls under bobby-pin Xs. Claire Coolidge works in a beauty parlor. "Calvin and Winifred!" she squealed.

Between Mrs. Coolidge and us, a dozen cats appeared. They swarmed Catman, hissing for position.

"Hi, Mrs. Coolidge!" I called.

She shuffled over and ran her fingers through my tangled hair. "What I wouldn't give for this head of hair!"

Lizzy came from the kitchen, holding a half-eaten tomato. Her hair looked as perfect as when she'd left for school, ten times better than my hair ever looked. "Hi, you two! Look, Winnie!" Lizzy pointed to the tomato. "After-school snack! Isn't that a great idea? Mrs. Coolidge says it's the forgotten fruit."

"Yours is in the kitchen!" Mrs. Coolidge assured me. "Calvin, show our guests to their quarters! Winnie, the west wing, second floor. Lizzy, east wing on third."

Lizzy and I exchanged looks of terror as we

followed Catman up the winding staircase, dodging cats that darted underfoot.

"We're used to staying in the same room, Catman," Lizzy confided.

Catman changed directions and led us down a long hall to a wooden door. It creaked when he pulled it open.

The room smelled minty, and everything in it was green, including the largest canopy bed I'd ever seen. I sat on it, and my feet didn't touch the floor. A small black cat with huge white paws pounced up and climbed into my lap.

"This cat has six toes!" I exclaimed, petting him.

"Six in front. Seven in back," Catman said. "Name's Bumby."

"Brumby? You named her after our English teacher?" Ms. Brumby would have a cow if she found out. And she would have hated that her namesake was two-colored. Ms. Brumby dressed in only one color from head to foot.

"Not Brumby. *Bumby*," Catman corrected. "In honor of Ernest Hemingway's famous six-toed Cuban cat. Hemingway's first son was also nick-named Bumby."

Lizzy ran to a corner of the room and pointed to a spiderweb. "Sweet!"

Catman grinned. "Thought you'd like that."

A phone rang downstairs. Seconds later Mrs. Coolidge shouted up the stairs, "Calvin! Girls! Help!"

We hurried to the top of the stairs.

"What's wrong?" Lizzy asked.

Mrs. Coolidge threw her hands in the air. "The Colonel just called! He's coming to dinner!"

Catman slid down the banister, and Lizzy and I took the stairs.

For the next hour Mrs. Coolidge buzzed around the kitchen like an Arabian in a snake pit. "Winnie, Kool-Aid! Lizzy, potatoes—the Colonel likes them undercooked. Thank goodness I have green Jell-O!"

The phone rang, and Mrs. Coolidge dropped a box of rigatoni. She lifted the receiver and knelt for the box. "Yes? They're right here! Just a moment!" She held the phone out to me.

I couldn't move. Something must have happened to Dad. I knew it.

Lizzy grabbed the phone. "Dad? Great! How's Chicago?"

I exhaled. *Thank you, God! Thank you!* Dad was okay. He was all right.

But as quickly as relief had come, it vanished. After all, Dad was in Chicago. Who knew what went on at the Invention Convention? And he'd still have to fly back.

Lizzy hadn't stopped chattering. ". . . bed the size of our living room! And our own bathroom! And Colonel Coolidge is coming to dinner!" She held the phone out to me. I shook my head. Lizzy kept talking. "What? Winnie? She's fine! She's . . . busy helping with dinner. . . . I'll tell her. Okay! Love you too! Bye!"

Lizzy hung up and raised her eyebrows at me. "Dad says hello and he loves you."

I joined Mrs. Coolidge. "Where's that Kool-Aid?"

Catman and I set the long dining table with good silver and two forks for everybody.

"I wish Bart would get home!" Mrs. Coolidge exclaimed, dumping a load of rigatoni into a pot of boiling water. "We'll have to finish dinner in time for the Colonel to make tonight's performance—in West Salem, isn't it?"

Catman set down tall wooden salt and

pepper shakers and announced, "The Colonel's here."

I ran to the window in time to see a big circus truck pull up.

The doorbell rang. Mrs. Coolidge raced toward the door until Lizzy stopped her. "Your robe?" Lizzy asked.

Mrs. Coolidge screamed, then darted up the staircase.

The doorbell rang again, hard and fast this time. Lizzy opened the door.

"And who might you be?" bellowed the Colonel.

Lizzy smiled. "Lizzy Willis. Pleased to meet you. Mrs. Coolidge will be right down. You know my sister, Winnie?" She nodded my way. She motioned him in and talked to him as if he were an old friend.

The cats stayed clear of the Colonel. Only the big, flat-faced Churchill tried to rub up against the Colonel's gray pant cuffs.

The Colonel shook him off. "Scat!"

"Churchill," Catman said. I didn't know if he was calling the cat or introducing him.

"Churchill?" Colonel Coolidge scoffed. "You named your cat after Winston Churchill? The

84

man was born in a ladies' room during a dance! What's wrong with *Eisenhower* for a name?"

Lizzy linked her arm through the Colonel's and moved him along. "So, Colonel, where was the circus last month?"

"Maine. Wonderful state, Maine! The only one-syllable state."

"Colonel!" Mrs. Coolidge called from the top of the staircase. She'd changed into a pink formal. Three-inch heels had replaced her slippers, and her hair had been freed from the bobby pins and now fell into dozens of ringlets.

The Colonel met her at the foot of the stairs, took her hand, and bowed. "Madame, you look stunning!"

She giggled.

He turned to us. "This lovely lady could have made an outstanding circus performer! I can't say the same of her husband. He lacked the discipline. Refused the Coolidge tradition of shining his boots every night!"

"Where *is* Bart?" she asked. "He should be home by now."

"Not a problem!" declared the Colonel. "Let's eat!"

We sat at the long table, with Catman and his mother at the ends. "Lizzy can pray," Catman suggested.

It would have been okay if we hadn't prayed. Lizzy and I know how to talk to God inside. I was pretty sure the Coolidges didn't pray before meals. But Catman knew we did, and it was cool of him to mention it.

Lizzy thanked God for the food, the circus, everybody at the table, and a lot of people— including Dad—who weren't.

She said, "Amen," and I opened my eyes in time to see salt and pepper shakers flying toward Mrs. Coolidge. She reached out and caught one in each hand.

"Sweet!" Lizzy exclaimed. "How did you do that?"

"The woman is a born performer!" the Colonel insisted. "Juggle, please!"

"But we shouldn't—," Mrs. Coolidge began.

"Proceed!" he demanded.

Mrs. Coolidge blew out one of the silver candles, grabbed the candlestick, and juggled it with the shakers. Then she tossed one after the other down the table to Catman. He juggled too, then fired them back to his mom. They kept it going, juggling back and forth without spilling a grain of salt.

Lizzy and I applauded.

Catman caught all three objects, set them down, and began to pass the food.

"How's that lovely young man Raymond?" Mrs. Coolidge asked.

"That boy takes all my time and half my energy!" roared the Colonel. "And his act is in disarray!"

I was thinking there must be more to Colonel Coolidge than met the eye. All these years he'd taken care of an orphan who wasn't really his relation.

By the time we got to dessert, Oreo cookies, the Colonel had told us half a dozen army stories. Some made me want to cry—like how Private Ayers lost one thumb to a land mine and his other thumb in a kitchen accident. Others made us laugh, like Lieutenant Daley, who married an army nurse three days before getting shipped to Germany. When she got assigned to a French base, Lieutenant Daley had gone AWOL, absent without leave, to see her. Private Ayers answered roll call for him, Sergeant Alden covered his duties, and Second

Lieutenant House loaned him a prisoner of war as his driver. "I should have put Daley in the brig for desertion!" barked the Colonel.

"Instead," Mrs. Coolidge added, eyes glimmering, "you let Lieutenant Daley use your Jeep!"

"Turns out the woman was well worth it," Colonel Coolidge put in. A cloud seemed to pass over his face. "Grand fellows. With the passing of Lieutenant Daley, we're down to the last four soldiers of the Fighting 44th."

I thought about how sad old people must get when most people their age have already died. The Colonel inspected his grape Kool-Aid, then chugged it.

"I've got the Kool-Aid for your canteen toast," Mrs. Coolidge said softly.

"Soldiers drink grape Kool-Aid from canteens?" Lizzy asked. "They don't teach us that in history books!"

"We of the Fighting 44th use it to toast our comrades who have gone before us," the Colonel explained.

"The Colonel kept his men's canteens," Mrs. Coolidge continued. "He only brings them out every five years. If a soldier has died since the last reunion, the others turn over his canteen and toast him."

Colonel Coolidge leaned back in his chair. "Only four upright canteens remain."

Mrs. Coolidge jumped up from the table and dashed to a small box that looked like a short video player. She popped in a square black thing.

"Eight-track tape," Catman whispered. "Before cassettes and CDs."

Mrs. Coolidge sat down and locked gazes with the Colonel. I knew a song filled with meaning was about to come on, maybe from World War II.

Then the music burst from the box:

Hang on Sloopy, Sloopy hang on
(Da-dum, Da-dum, Da-dum, Da-dum)
Hang on Sloopy, Sloopy hang on

The silly rock and roll wasn't what I'd expected. But Mrs. Coolidge and the Colonel listened solemnly, while Catman bobbed his head to the beat.

Lizzy and I made faces at each other. She obviously didn't get it either.

When the song ended, after a million *Sloopy*

hang ons, the Colonel dabbed the corner of his eye with his napkin. "Bart's daddy, my son Carter, God rest his soul, loved that song."

"Calvin," commanded his mother, "tell them how Carter Coolidge made 'Hang On Sloopy' the official state rock song of Ohio."

Catman swallowed the last Oreo whole, then recited: "House Resolution No. 16, the 116th General Assembly of Ohio, 1985: 'Whereas "Hang On Sloopy" is of particular relevance to members of the Baby Boom Generation, who were once dismissed as a bunch of longhaired, crazy kids, but who now are old enough and vote in sufficient numbers to be taken quite seriously—' "

Colonel Coolidge held up his hand, as if he couldn't bear to hear more.

And I hadn't even known Ohio had a state rock song.

Just then Bart Coolidge burst through the door, panting. "Colonel! Sorry I'm late! It took some doing to get that trailer you asked for, but we had one on the back lot."

Usually Bart Coolidge is jolly, ready with a corny used-car joke. And when he comes home, he rushes to his wife and kisses her as if they haven't seen each other for years. But now he just glanced sheepishly at her. Apparently the Colonel didn't like mushy stuff any better than he liked lawn ornaments. I thought of Romeo and Juliet.

"I'm starved!" Bart announced.

The Colonel threw his napkin onto his plate. "Let's go!"

"Go?" Bart repeated. "But I haven't eaten."

"Gluttony is a sin! That extra weight may have kept you off the high wire!" Colonel Coolidge slipped his jacket back on and strode to the door.

"Good luck at the circus tonight!" I called.

The Colonel wheeled around. "Don't just sit there! And *you*–" he pointed at Bart–"take this girl to her horse! They shall perform this very night!"

innie!" Lizzy shook my chair. "They're waiting for you!"

I hadn't budged since Colonel Coolidge said Nickers and I were performing tonight. "But he said we'd be *Ashland* greeters. We're not ready yet!"

"Nonsense!" the Colonel shouted from the door. "We need you tonight!"

"Can't argue with the Colonel," Catman whispered.

Bart Coolidge drove the used trailer to my barn. Nickers wasn't crazy about stepping in. My Arabian used to be called Wild Thing, and now I remembered why. It took a handful of oats, four false starts, and lots of sweet-talking to get her loaded.

93

The whole circus had moved overnight to West Salem, a small town about 10 miles east of Ashland. Nickers snorted and pawed the ground when I unloaded her.

Catman's dad wandered off, and I led Nickers through the midway to get her used to the lights and noises. Her ears flicked as we passed vendors, screaming teens, and sideshow acts. I recognized Gabrielle, dressed in a jungle costume, holding a giant python, and calling herself The Snake Lady. And Dinglehopper was a barker, shouting, "Step right up! Get your tickets here!"

"Keep your eye on that sneaky clown," I whispered to Nickers.

"Mommy! Look at that beautiful horse!" a little boy screamed, pointing at Nickers.

I smiled at him, so proud of my horse. She *was* beautiful.

Before long, Nickers settled down, and I led her behind the menagerie tent to rehearse. She did every trick perfectly . . . except the bow. I knew it was crazy to still care so much about

94

getting Nickers to bow. Dad and Lizzy wouldn't even be there for Mom's birthday. But I couldn't let it go. I wanted it to be my birthday present to Mom. She always opened and closed with a bow.

Ramon trotted up on Midnight and slid off. His black stallion pranced in place and pulled at the bridle. Nickers arched her neck and snorted.

"Your horse is beautiful!" Ramon shouted, struggling to hold on to Midnight.

"Thanks! What's with Midnight?"

"You're asking *me?*" Ramon scratched his horse on the neck, and Midnight quieted a bit. "I just fed him and walked him around. I hope he's not too jumpy to get through the acts."

Lizzy ran up, with Catman trailing behind. "Winnie! This is so exciting! I can't believe you're actually in the circus! With elephants and clowns and—" Lizzy stopped and stared at Ramon.

He grinned at her. "Either I'm seeing double, or this is your twin."

I sighed. "Ramon, this is my *little* sister, Lizzy. Lizzy, I told you about Ramon."

Ramon led Midnight closer, as if he meant to shake Lizzy's hand.

Lizzy squealed and stepped back. "Sorry. Horses make me nervous."

Ramon laughed. "Guess you're *not* twins!"

Catman and Lizzy left to get good seats, and Ramon and I took the horses into the menagerie tent.

Gabrielle rushed by and shoved a bag at me. "Colonel said to give you this. Put it on. Greeting starts in five minutes."

"Don't mind Gabrielle," Ramon said, after she'd left and we'd settled our horses into stalls. "It's tough sharing the ring with an elephant and a camel, especially when the elephant gets most of the applause."

Ramon had me change in the Colonel's trailer, which he and the Colonel shared. I was surprised how houselike it looked inside, with couches and chairs and a TV. On a wooden table sat the army canteens Catman had told us about, 12 upside down, four still standing upright. It made me sad, like seeing a flag at half-mast. I thought about my family's table and imagined four canteens set out, three up, one down.

I hurried to the bathroom and put on the white ballerina-like outfit, white tights, and white

96

slippers that were too big. I kept my back to the mirror so I wouldn't have to see myself. How could I possibly go out there in this getup?

I stayed in the bathroom until Ramon knocked on the trailer door. "Winnie! Time to go!"

I took a deep breath and faced the mirror. For a minute, I wasn't sure it was me. My hair was still straggling out of my braid, and my freckles hadn't gone anywhere. But the rest of me looked like a circus performer. Gold glittered from the high neck of the ballet dress. It fit snug down to my waist, then spread out to my knees.

Ramon held the door as I stepped out of the trailer. "Wow!"

My face burned. I hoped he couldn't see me blush.

As I led Nickers into the Big Top, I could feel people staring. Kids pointed at Nickers. Gabrielle and her mom were working the spectators on one side, Barker and the clowns the other.

"Go, Winnie! Sweet!" Lizzy cheered from the stand. She and Mrs. Barker waved. Catman gave me the peace sign.

I closed my eyes, hearing voices and noise roaring in my ears. *God, I can't do this! Why did I come here? Why did Dad have to leave?*

Nickers nuzzled my neck. It felt like an answer, like God saying, *You know Nickers and I are with you. Can't be that bad.*

"Look at her!"

I opened my eyes to see a little girl, maybe five years old, holding her mom's hand and pointing at me.

"What's your name?" I asked, my voice raspy. Lizzy says she wishes she had my "unique" voice, but I cleared my throat.

The girl moved closer to her mother, but her big brother answered for her. "Ashley."

I nodded. "Nickers, are you glad Ashley came to the circus?"

I moved my finger toward Nickers' chest, and she nodded yes.

Ashley and her brother laughed.

"Should these guys go to bed early tonight?" I asked, moving my hand to Nickers' withers.

Nickers shook her head no.

The parents clapped for us before taking their seats. Barker ran over and told me what a great job I was doing.

I repeated my "act" four times. Then Lizzy called me over, and I "worked" their section of the bleachers. Nickers shook hands, answered questions, and counted. I wished Dad were here to see us.

The ringmaster blew his whistle. Ramon gave me the high-five sign as I fell in behind him for the parade.

A white Lipizzan galloped past and cut in line. Gabrielle shouted through her fake smile, "Know your place, cowgirl!"

She *had* to be related to Summer.

When the parade ended, I stabled Nickers in the menagerie tent, put my real clothes back on, and raced to the bleachers to sit with Lizzy and Catman.

"You guys rock!" Lizzy exclaimed before running off to sit with friends.

I glanced at Catman, but he was too hypno- tized by the lion act to even notice me. During the next few acts, I did my best to keep my eye on Dinglehopper.

"Give it a rest. Dinglehopper didn't do it," Catman said, as Gabrielle's family finished their act with the star elephant.

"Catman, I ran an Internet search on that man. Dinglehopper doesn't exist!"

"That's because *James D. Hopkins* is an ex-con."

I gasped. "We have to tell the Colonel!"

"He knows. Hopkins has been clowning with the Colonel for 15 years. He hates kids, and he doesn't groove on Barker. But the dude's solid."

I had to admit that Catman is a good judge of character. Still, he's no detective. Ramon's big chance was only four days away. No way would I stop watching my number one suspect just because Catman liked him.

Ramon and Midnight's first act went okay, but they skipped a couple of tricks, probably because Midnight was so jumpy. I *had* to figure out why.

Something was nagging me, but I couldn't put my finger on it. Was it something I'd seen? something I'd heard? something—

"I got it!" I cried.

Catman shot me a what-is-it-this-time look.

I dragged him to the exit and waited for Ramon to finish. "The Pet Help Line, Catman!" I whispered. "That's what I've been trying to think of! I had an e-mail from a girl whose horse sounded just like Midnight—jumpy and hyper."

Ramon cantered up and hopped off Midnight. "I give up!" He sounded more frustrated than ever. "It was all I could do to control

Midnight in there! What made me think I could make it in a bigger circus? I'm lucky the Colonel doesn't fire me!"

"Ramon!" I shouted. "What have you been feeding Midnight?"

"Huh?" He looked at Catman, who shrugged. "I don't know. The Colonel buys it. I give it to Midnight."

"Show me where the feed's stored!" I demanded.

We followed Ramon to the menagerie tent, and he tied up Midnight next to Nickers. Then he led us to a row of bins in the back. They looked like plastic trash cans. Ramon pointed to the one marked *Coolidge.* "That's Midnight's."

I lifted the lid, dipped out a handful of mixed, moist grain, and sniffed. "Molasses, sugar beet, and barley, with rolled oats!"

"Far out!" Catman commented.

Ramon paced, shaking his head. "I thought it looked different than usual! Is something wrong with it?"

"Not if you're a racehorse or an old horse who needs extra energy," I explained. "But for Midnight, yeah! It's too rich! No wonder he's jumpy!"

"But why would the Colonel buy it?" Ramon asked.

"Maybe he didn't." I reached my arm deep into the can and came out with a handful of regular oats. Moving to the other bins, I lifted the lids, one by one. The three bins next to Midnight's held regular oats.

Only one bin remained, the one marked *LeBlond*. I pulled off the lid.

Nothing but oats.

"I was so sure I'd find the energy feed!" I replaced the lid. The bin scooted, and I caught a glimpse of something behind it, a half-empty feed sack. I pulled it out and read the label: *Senior Feed—High-Energy Mix*.

"There's your answer!" I shouted. "Someone dumped *this* high-octane feed on top of Midnight's regular oats! And no way was it an accident!"

Catman inspected the sack while I smelled a handful of the grain. "It's the same feed as Midnight's!" I exclaimed.

"What do you think you're doing?" Gabrielle LeBlond stormed down the stalls toward us.

I stood up and braced myself. "We're solving a mystery. Does this feed belong to you?"

Her pale face looked sunburned with rage. "Yes! Get away from there!" She started for me, but Ramon stepped between us.

"Gabrielle?" He sounded hurt, not angry. "Why did you buy it?"

"For Chaparral—not that it's any of your business!" She glared at us.

Catman whispered to me, "Old horse."

"Chaparral's the only horse around here who

103

needs special feed!" Gabrielle snapped. "So just keep your paws off!"

"Later, man," Catman said. "Sorry."

"Sorry?" I repeated.

Catman nearly dragged me out of the tent.

Ramon followed. "I feel lousy for accusing her. Poor Gabrielle!"

"Poor Gabrielle?" I couldn't believe these guys! Just because she was pretty—okay, gorgeous. "Are you crazy? Okay, maybe the feed *is* for the old Lipizzan. That still doesn't explain how it got into Midnight's bin! Gabrielle probably put it there! She's jealous of you, Ramon!"

"Any cat could make that feed scene," Catman said.

"Maybe it was a mistake," Ramon suggested.

Note to self: Don't waste your breath trying to reason with boys!

Gabrielle may have fooled them, but she didn't fool me. For all I knew, she was in cahoots with Dinglehopper. So it was up to me to protect Midnight Mystery. "Ramon, make sure Midnight gets plain oats for now on. Mix it with a tablespoon of oil for a couple of days to calm him."

I turned to Catman. "As for me, I'll be keep-

ing my eye on Dinglehopper *and* Gabrielle
LeBlond!"

That night, after the circus was over, I settled
Nickers back in her own barn, and Mr. Coolidge
drove us back to Coolidge Castle. Mrs. Coolidge, still in her dinner gown, was asleep in
front of the TV. Mr. Coolidge picked her up
like a baby and carried her upstairs.

Alone downstairs, I listened to the house, the
way it creaked and moaned in the wind. Branches
scratched the windows like they wanted in.

I missed my dad. It felt like he was as far
away as Mom, like I'd never see him again
either. And things would never, ever be the
same.

Tuesday morning I climbed into jeans and two
sweatshirts and walked to my barn for chores.
Nickers greeted me with a whinny that shot
frost clouds into the still-dark morning.

I mucked stalls and groomed Towaco and Nickers, cleaning out their hooves and brushing the fuzz off their early winter coats. It was a great way to start the day, even though I could have curled up in the haystack with Nelson, my barn cat, and slept all morning.

Before heading back, I tried to get Nickers to bow. But she just didn't want to.

Back at the Coolidges' I found Mr. Coolidge at the kitchen counter cutting out something from the newspaper. "Morning, Winnie!" He straightened his hairpiece with one hand and brushed crumbs off his Tweety Bird tie with the other. "Sa-a-ay! What did the Volvo say to the Volkswagen when the little girl changed the VW's flat tire in 30 seconds flat?"

I couldn't help laughing before he reached the punch line. "I give up, Mr. Coolidge."

"'I declare, you do *tire* easily!' Get it?" He laughed in short huffs like a horse's neighs. "I must finish this contest entry. Help yourself to cereal."

"Morning!" Lizzy sang, bouncing into the

kitchen. Her hair looked perfect and so did her shirt and vest, even though she'd had them since Iowa.

Mrs. Coolidge stumbled in, her hair piled high as a beehive. She wore a purple-and-white flowered dress with a wide, gold belt. She kissed her husband, then plopped on the stool next to him and read over his shoulder. "Smidgen . . . maple . . . establishment."

"That's it!" Mr. Coolidge scribbled onto the entry form. "You're a genius with word scrambles, Mrs. Coolidge!"

"And *you* with jingles, Mr. Coolidge!" She straightened his hairpiece. "Morning, girls!" She made a sweeping gesture at the cupboards. "Have some cereal!"

I opened the cupboard above the sink. Five shelves were packed with cereal boxes, all the same brand of sugared oat flakes. A cardboard rectangle was missing from the back of each box.

Lizzy opened the next cupboard. More identical boxes. Two more cupboards revealed the same thing.

"Contest entries." Catman had slipped in catlike. He took down a box. "They're into contests."

"Mr. Coolidge won that blender!" Mrs. Coolidge said, pointing to the unopened box on the counter. "And 17 others like it. Plus all-expense-paid vacations to Paris, Texas; Versailles, Missouri; Florence, Utah; and Rome, Mississippi!"

"True," her husband admitted, "but *you* won the year's supply of cat food—lasted three days in this household." He frowned at Wilhemina, the fat, orange tabby, and Cat Burglar, the longhaired white cat with black-mask markings.

"You guys rock!" Lizzy exclaimed, pouring us bowls of cereal.

When the flakes didn't crunch, I wondered how long ago their contest had run.

The phone rang. Mr. Coolidge grabbed it on the first ring. "Jack! How's Chicago?"

Lizzy and I glanced at each other. Then she ran to the phone and took it. "Dad! How are you? Did you find Zack? It's so noisy there! I can hardly hear you!"

I walked over and pressed my ear to the receiver. When Dad spoke, I held my breath.

"I'm on the floor of the Invention Convention!" Dad shouted. "I've seen 176 different mousetraps! And a motorized porch swing, an automatic clothes brush, and a combination cheese-grater/onion-slicer/cockroach-catcher!"

"Ask him when he's coming home!" I whispered.

"What's that?" Dad shouted. "Did—?" Laughter exploded, drowning out his voice.

"When are you coming home?" Lizzy shouted.

"Sunday! Saturday night if—" But his voice was swallowed by other voices.

I couldn't stand it. I walked back to my cereal and tried to get it to go past the lump in my throat.

Lizzy shouted for a while, then gave up. "Love you, Dad!" She sat back down. "Dad said two companies asked about his back bike! And he met a woman who invented hot-air socks."

"Don't you girls worry about your father!" Mrs. Coolidge put in. "He's having the time of his life!"

Which was exactly what I was worried about.

Mrs. Coolidge sidled behind me and fiddled with my hair. "Hair like this is a gift!" She disappeared and returned with a long-handled comb. "All you need is height!" She held up strands of my hair and combed from the ends to the roots. "In the business, we call this teasing!"

Teasing hurt.

Lizzy's lips twitched, like she was fighting to hold in a laugh. "I have to go. Thanks for breakfast. See you, Winnie!" She dashed out like the kitchen was on fire.

Catman finished his third bowl of flakes, said *"Ciao,"* and left me stranded.

As soon as I could get out of Mrs. Coolidge's clutches, I headed out on my back bike. As I pedaled backward onto the street, two kids pointed at me. I would have thought the town was used to my weird bike by now. Dad had sold six back bikes in Ashland. Nobody ever laughed at Catman's.

More heads turned the closer I got to school. *Maybe they saw me in the circus!* I wondered if this was what Ramon went through all the time.

I parked my bike as M, dressed in black, strolled by. He shook his head and kept going.

"What are you supposed to be?" Brian yelled. "Did Halloween come late to the Willises?" Next to Brian, Hawk stared at me as she pointed to her head.

I felt for my head and was shocked to touch hair—big hair where no hair should have been. I tried to push it down, but like a bubble, it bulged at the sides. When I let go, it bounced up again.

Folding my arms over my head, I darted up the stairs, ignoring the laughter of Summer and her groupies. In the bathroom I stuck my head under cold water until it soaked through the tangles.

Sal came in and stood next to me. "Totally not you."

"Totally not *anybody!*" I muttered as the bathroom emptied and the bell rang.

I kept soaking my hair until I could squish it down. With brute force I separated my hair into three strands and braided it. For the rest of the day, I looked like a drowned rat. But it was better than being a walking beehive.

After school I did my homework at Pat's Pets while I waited for my turn on the help line. I answered three horse e-mails and was on my way out when Hawk walked in. All day I'd wanted to talk to her about the circus. But she's a hundred times harder to talk to in school.

"Howdy, Hawk!" Pat hollered, coming toward

us. "Winnie, Bart called and asked if I'd drive you and Nickers to the circus. We can leave in two shakes of a lamb's tail, if you're game. No offense!" she added to imaginary lambs.

I turned to Hawk. "Come with us, Hawk!"

Victoria Hawkins has mastered the art of not showing her emotions. She claims it's part of her American Indian heritage and calls it "inscrutable," which means "impossible to figure out." Pat and I waited for her answer.

"Yes," Hawk agreed. "Thank you."

Nickers loaded easily this time. On the drive over, I filled Pat and Hawk in on my two prime suspects in the circus mystery: Jimmy Green Dinglehopper and Gabrielle LeBlond. "I'm afraid if I can't figure out who's trying to wreck the circus, something awful's going to happen." Inside I had an ocean of worry, with waves splashing back and forth from Dad to Ramon to Midnight and even to Nickers.

"You be careful now!" Pat warned as she dropped us off at the circus entrance. "I'll be back soon as I can!"

Keeping an eye out for anything suspicious, I strolled the midway with Nickers and Hawk. We passed the lion cages and saw Dinglehopper hanging out with Leopold.

"The short guy is the lion tamer," I whispered to Hawk. "He can't talk. The tall, red-haired one is Dinglehopper, the clown who hates Barker."

"I will help you watch them, Winnie," Hawk promised.

We found Ramon and Midnight outside the menagerie tent. Ramon talked with Hawk while I examined Midnight hoof to muzzle. "He seems calmer, don't you think, Ramon?" I stroked Midnight's neck and blew into his nostrils. His big, brown eyes shut as he rested his chin on my shoulder. I *had* to find out who was trying to hurt this beautiful stallion.

Ramon stabled Midnight and came back to help me work with Nickers. He tried his hand at getting Nickers to bow until I could tell my horse had had enough.

I'd just called it quits when Catman appeared with an armful of hot dogs. He passed them out to us, then started on his own—bun first, dog last.

Before I could take a bite of my hot dog,

Nickers nuzzled it. I wasn't hungry anyway.
"Be my guest."

Nickers took a whiff of the mustard. Her lips curled instantly into what looked like a big horse laugh.

"It seems as if Nickers has learned a new trick," Hawk observed.

While the rest of them ate, I taught Nickers to "laugh" every time I raised my mustard-dipped pinkie. She's so smart that she mastered it in 15 minutes.

Two jugglers and the whole trapeze act stopped by to see how Ramon was doing. A few yards away Gabrielle was working with her Lipizzaner, but I could tell she was watching us.

Finally, she stormed past us, left her horse in the tent, and stomped out again.

"Gabrielle!" Ramon called. "Come meet Hawk—"

Gabrielle kept going as if she hadn't heard Ramon.

"Hawk, I'll catch you later in the Big Top!" I ran after Gabrielle, ducking behind tents, staying out of sight as I trailed her all the way to the Colonel's trailer.

She banged on the door. When it opened, she barged in.

I sneaked up, quiet as Catman, and listened at the door.

"It's not fair!" Gabrielle yelled.

"We've been over this a thousand times!" barked the Colonel. "Ramon and Midnight Mystery are my top act!"

"Haven't you been watching your own circus lately?" she demanded. "They're not cutting it! They'll give the circus a bad name. You *know* my dancing-horse act is exactly what you need! And I can handle the trick act, too!"

Colonel Coolidge sighed. "You really want Ramon's job, don't you?"

"What I want is a chance to prove this circus will be better off if you give me the lead horse acts!"

"Well . . ." The Colonel sounded tired, on the verge of giving up. "You just may get your chance if Ramon can't get his horse under control."

"Good! I'll hold you to that!" Gabrielle stormed out the door, shoving it so hard it banged my head.

I watched her goose-step away, and a shiver of fear shot through me. Gabrielle LeBlond wanted Ramon's job, and she'd do whatever it took to get it!

$\mathcal{I}$ kept an eye on Gabrielle until I had to get
ready for the show. In the Big Top, Nickers was
a bigger hit than ever with her mustard laugh.
I'd have given anything to have Dad in the
bleachers to see it.

To give Ramon more time between his acts,
Colonel Coolidge had bumped the trick-horse
act to second slot, behind the lions. I stood
guard ringside and could still hear Catman
cheering from the stands during the lion act.

The second Leopold finished, three men ran
out and rolled the cages out of the ring while
the Colonel announced, "Ramon and the
Magnificent Midnight Mystery!"

The black stallion galloped twice around the
ring before heading to the center. Gabrielle

117

wasn't in the Big Top, and I'd started to relax when Midnight squealed and skidded to a stop. Ramon tried to get him to go, but the stallion reared. Somehow Ramon got him down and pulled him in a circle before aiming for the center again. Midnight balked, legs stiff.

I wanted to run out and help, but I knew it wouldn't do any good. Midnight's eyes shone with fear, too much fear for me to talk him out of it.

The Colonel waved his top hat, signaling the band to play. Into the mike, he announced, "While Midnight Mystery makes up his mind, will you cast your gaze on the far ring, where the Amazing Ming Family will juggle like you've never seen before!"

The Mings scrambled for props and raced out to do their act.

I ran to the center ring as Ramon slid off Midnight. "Winnie, what's the matter with this horse? He's never balked, never refused to do a show!"

Catman appeared. "Funky." He frowned, then walked to the center of the ring.

I followed him as he went straight to a clump of brown in the sawdust. "Cats," he muttered.

I knelt down and inspected the dry, brown lump. "Catman, is it—?"

"Old lion dung," he answered.

Jimmy Dinglehopper and another clown trotted in and began sweeping the ring.

I wheeled around to Ramon. "No wonder Midnight wouldn't go near here! Horses fear lions more than anything in the world! No horse would go near lion dung!" I turned to Catman. "I smell Gabrielle LeBlond! She knows enough about horses to know this lion dung would wreck Ramon's act for sure!"

My head buzzed with anger. "That does it! This all stops right now!" I stormed past Ramon and Midnight and out of the Big Top. Gabrielle couldn't be far away.

I found her behind the tent, sitting on her Lipizzaner and doing the exact same bow Ramon did to finish his act.

"Gabrielle!" I shouted, charging at her. "I know it was you! You'd do anything to hurt Ramon and Midnight!"

She jumped off her horse and looked ready to attack.

Catman strolled between us. "What's happening?"

"I don't need to mess up Ramon's act! He's doing that on his own!" Gabrielle snapped. "I have my own act! And a champion horse that's wasted here! *And I* can ride bareback, without half the trappings Ramon needs! Do you see any fancy saddles on my horse? Russian and American trick riders need saddles. Not me! No props. Nothing but this!" She pointed to a white strap that circled her horse's belly like a wide belt. "All I use is this surcingle!" She unbuckled it and threw it at us. Catman caught it. It looked like a leather cinch with handles.

"Sooner or later the Colonel will come to his senses and make me the star of this show! Now, if you'll excuse me, I have a performance!" Gabrielle grabbed the surcingle out of Catman's hands and stormed off.

Hawk, Catman, and I sat on the front row for the LeBlonds' act.

"Gabrielle's stallion is beautiful and well trained," Hawk said, as the Lipizzaner pranced in step with the elephant and camel. "Are you sure she is behind all the circus problems?"

"Yes!" I snapped. Hawk was as bad as Catman and Ramon.

Near the end of the act Mrs. LeBlond exited first, leaving Gabrielle on her horse and Mr. LeBlond on the elephant. As usual, the Lipizzaner reared, and Gabrielle waved good-bye so the elephant could gather final applause.

The Lipizzaner pawed the air. I heard a snap. And Gabrielle fell sideways off her horse.

The crowd gasped. Her mother screamed.

Catman and I started out to the ring, where Gabrielle lay in the dust. I saw the surcingle lying on the ground beside her.

Before we reached her, Gabrielle did a somersault, bounded to her feet, and leaped onto her horse bareback. She moved so swiftly, it almost looked like part of her act. I wondered if I could have pulled it off. I found myself clapping as loud as everybody else in the audience.

While Gabrielle circled the Big Top on her horse, Catman strode over and picked up the surcingle. He stared at it as he walked back and showed it to me. The strap was still buckled, but the belt had broken in two.

"Freaky." Catman pointed to the ends of the

broken leather. It was a straight, smooth cut. Even though the whole belt looked cracked and worn, the break was clean and sharp.

"Somebody cut it, Catman!" I cried. "It wasn't an accident!" I thought about all the rotten things I'd said to Gabrielle. How could I have been so wrong? Somebody was trying to hurt her too.

Catman didn't say anything. I stared at him, amazed that his expression hadn't changed one bit. Didn't he get it? "Catman, don't you see what this means? Somebody cut Gabrielle's surcingle on purpose! There's a madman loose around here! And nobody's going to be safe until we find out who it is!"

Hawk and Catman convinced me to sit back down in the bleachers until the show was over. I wanted to do something, to investigate. As I stared blankly at the trapeze act, I tried to get my brain to pull up photos of things I'd observed around the circus over the past few days.

But it didn't work. It never does when I want it to. What good is a photographic memory if you can't choose the memories?

When Ramon rode out for the cossack act, I felt like a horse with colic. I thought I'd hurl. The act went okay, but it lacked energy. It

122

wasn't Midnight's fault. This time it was Ramon's. He kept looking over his shoulder, as if waiting for something awful to happen.

Who could blame him?

I kept going over every circus accident, trying to come up with clues that shouldn't have led me to Gabrielle. The burr under Midnight's saddle. The flash of light on his face. The wrong feed in his bin. The lion dung. Now Gabrielle's broken surcingle.

It wasn't until Barker waved up at us that I felt my brain kick in. *Barker. Clown. Dinglehopper!* I'd seen something that wasn't right. What was it? I tried to remember. I pictured Hawk and me strolling the midway with Nickers. We saw Gabrielle as the Snake Lady, Ramon and Midnight. And . . .

Then I remembered. The lion cages! We'd seen Dinglehopper and Leopold doing something at the cages! But what? Not talking! That was for sure! Catman himself had told me Leopold didn't talk.

"I know who's behind everything!" I whispered, already on the move out of the bleachers.

Hawk followed me. "Winnie, who? Not Gabrielle."

I turned and frowned. She had to rub it in. "Of course not."

"Is it the clown then? Your other suspect?" she asked.

I didn't answer. I hadn't actually decided if Dinglehopper or Leopold was the real criminal. Maybe both of them! Ramon had followed the lion act. Leopold could easily have managed to leave the lion dung for Midnight to find. And Dinglehopper had come along afterward to sweep up the evidence.

We found the lion tamer back by the cages. "Hey, Leopold." I forced myself to swallow my famous temper. "I was wondering, what do you think would happen if, say, some lion dung was left in the arena? Like maybe just before a horse act?" If I could come at him sideways, he might give something away.

"Winnie?" Hawk whispered. She stood at my elbow, towering over both Leopold and me. "You said he cannot talk."

I frowned at Leopold. I knew he understood. Catman hadn't said anything about the lion tamer's hearing. But he looked bored with the whole thing, especially with me.

Catman streaked by us, dropped to the

ground, and rolled under the cages. In a few
seconds he rolled back out. "Hole."

Now it was Leopold's turn to frown.

Catman explained. "Some cat cut a hole in
the bottom of the cage. Dung dropped out."

Leopold dove under the cage to see for
himself.

I started to say something, but Catman
slipped between Hawk and me, looped his arms
through ours, and turned us back toward the Big
Top. "Leo's not your man."

I let myself be led by Catman until we were
halfway to the Big Top. Then I put on my
brakes. "You don't know Leopold's not guilty.
I'm going back." Why should I take Catman's
word that I had the wrong man? So he had a
hole in his cage. He could have put it there
himself!

Catman shrugged and kept walking. Hawk
went with him.

I jogged back to the cages.

Leopold's back was turned when I walked up.
I heard a deep voice and stopped to listen.
"They're all stupid, baby! Only you and me's got
the sense we was born with." Leopold the lion
tamer was talking! He was probably on a cell

phone, more than likely talking to his accomplice.

"You *can* talk!" I cried.

Slowly he turned his head and looked over his shoulder at me. What I saw in his black eyes made me wish I'd never come looking for him alone.

eave me alone!" growled Leopold, showing his jagged yellow teeth.

But I couldn't leave. I couldn't move.

He wheeled around to face me. Instead of a cell phone, he held a lion cub. He'd been talking to the lion?

"Go!" he yelled.

"B-but . . ." My throat had gone bone dry. "Catman . . . said you can't talk!"

He lowered his voice and spoke to his cub. "See how stupid they are?" When he glared up at me, his voice returned to a roar. "He didn't say I *can't* talk. He said I *don't* talk. Why? Because humans are too stupid to listen! That's why!"

"I agree. . . ." I tried to smile as I backed away.

"I don't like talking to humans either. Really I don't."

I turned and ran back to the Big Top. Maybe Catman was right about Leopold. Maybe he wasn't. But if Leopold hadn't sabotaged the circus and if Gabrielle hadn't done it either, I was back to Dinglehopper. And I'd already been there. Which meant I was going in circles and running out of time.

Wednesday the circus took a rare day off. I felt relieved. It gave me a whole day to think through the events of the week. I wanted to solve the mystery before the circus opened in Ashland Thursday night.

After school I manned the help line at Pat's Pets, then biked to the barn and took a short ride on Nickers before getting back to work on the bow. I'd just led Nickers out to the paddock behind the barn when the circus truck pulled up. Ramon got out of the driver's side.

"Back here!" I shouted.

He waved, then walked to the barn, hands in his pockets. When he came out of the barn into the paddock, he was holding my barn cat, a black cat with one white paw. Nelson is Churchill's kitten. Catman named the cat Nelson because that's what Winston Churchill named his cat.

"Catman said I'd find you here and gave me directions. The Colonel let me have the afternoon off. Amazing, huh?" He held up Nelson so I could pet him. Nickers nuzzled the cat, who's really as much hers as mine. "Tell me you're not still working on that bow."

"I think Nickers is getting closer to bowing," I said, not really sure if it was true.

"Why don't you forget about the bow?" Ramon set down the squirming Nelson. "Nickers' horse laugh is a better greeting trick anyway."

"I can't forget about it!" I snapped.

Ramon raised his eyebrows. "Sorry! I just meant you don't have to do it if—"

"I *do* have to do it! Nickers is going to bow! And she's going to do it by Friday! And if you don't believe me, then you can—!" I stopped. My throat burned and my eyes blurred. I stared at Nickers' hooves so Ramon couldn't see how close I was to crying. My temper was like a rodeo bronco just waiting for that gate to swing open. I was mad at Dad for not coming home for Mom's birthday. But I had no right to take it out on Ramon. "Sorry, Ramon." I looked up.

Ramon was scratching Nickers' cheek. "Want to tell me about it?" he asked.

When I didn't say anything, Ramon kept talking. "You have a great thing going here, Winnie the Horse Gentler. I envy you."

Me? You're the famous Ramon! Soon to star in the Beatty Show!"

He sighed. "I don't know, Winnie. I'm thinking maybe I won't even try the cossack act in Ashland."

"But you *have* to!" I insisted. "It means so much to you!"

Ramon narrowed his eyes at me.

I looked down again. "Catman told me about your mother." I moved closer and scratched Nickers' other cheek. "I understand, Ramon. You want to star in the circus she starred in." I could almost feel how much he wanted it, as much as I wanted to put on the birthday show the way Mom used to.

Ramon shook his head. "You couldn't possibly understand, Winnie."

"But I do." It felt like we were hanging on to the same cliff, trying to get back on solid ground however we could. "You need to ride in that circus for the same reason I need to get Nickers to bow by Friday." And then I told him. Every- thing. About Mom's birthday horse shows, Dad's Invention Convention, and the accident. And when I was done, he told me everything about his mother, all the stories the Colonel had told him about her in the Beatty Show.

"So I guess," Ramon concluded, "we both have a lot of work to do before Friday."

I nodded. Then I shivered. The temperature must have dropped 20 degrees since we'd been standing there.

Ramon glanced at his watch. "Man, I better get us both to the Coolidges' or the Colonel will serve our heads on a platter!"

"The Colonel?" I asked, jogging into the barn after Ramon.

"Didn't I tell you? The Colonel and I are invited to Coolidge Castle for dinner—and you and I are about to be late!"

Bart Coolidge, in Bermuda shorts, Hawaiian shirt, and a big white chef's hat, was leaning over a flaming barbeque grill outside his house, where lawn ornaments should have been.

"Sa-a-ay!" he hollered at us. "Ramon! Why did the Honda cross the street?"

Lizzy walked out in a ski jacket and mittens. "Hi, Winnie! How was school? I checked on Larry and the lizards, and they're all fine. Ramon, how's that horse? Isn't Mr. Coolidge amazing? Mrs. Coolidge says he barbeques all winter, dressed just like that." Lizzy glanced at the sky. "It's going to rain—storm even—with lightning, but not for hours yet."

Poor Mr. Coolidge couldn't squeeze in his punch line with my sister chattering.

Ramon squinted at the cloudless sky. "Doesn't look like rain to me."

"Lizzy's never wrong about weather," I said.

The Colonel was already seated when we walked inside. We scarfed down every hamburger and finished off Lizzy's broccoli casserole, which she'd sculpted in the shape of a circus tent, complete with a yellow flag on top. She'd even used cookie cutters to shape green Jell-O into giraffes, elephants, and tigers.

To the tune of eight-tracks playing in the background, Colonel Coolidge talked about his army buddies and explained more of the grape Kool-Aid tradition. "Sergeant Alden and Private Ayers had taken a German officer prisoner. We knew Hitler's forces were planning to attack that night, and we figured this officer knew where. After we'd tried every sort of persuasion allowed by the Geneva convention, I had an idea.

"'Lieutenant,' I said, 'this officer is of no use. Give him *the potion.*' Well, Lieutenant Daley read the situation immediately and played along. 'Not *the potion!*' he protested. The others joined in, holding their throats or looking away, while the German officer demanded to know what was happening.

"Second Lieutenant House filled a canteen with water, while Lieutenant Daley slowly ripped the top off a package of grape Kool-Aid my missus had sent that very day. Alden dumped in sugar, and I shook the canteen as the German officer pleaded with us not to make him drink *the potion.* In the end, he *spilled* the hour and location of the invasion." The Colonel grinned at Ramon as he took a sip of his Kool-Aid.

Mrs. Coolidge clinked her glass to her husband's. "And grape Kool-Aid may have saved hundreds of lives." She set down her long-stemmed glass and passed green Jell-O giraffes to Ramon. "Lizzy says the Beatty Show is scouting your act, Ramon. You must be so excited!"

The Colonel harrumphed.

"I just hope we find out who's sabotaging the circus before Friday," Ramon said, taking two giraffes and an elephant.

"Bosh and poppycock!" Colonel Coolidge slammed down his fork. "Someone is always trying to close my show or buy me out! 'Times are changing,' they say. Well, not for Colonel Coolidge *or* his circus! I shall never surrender!" He sat back and refolded his napkin. "Forget this other business, Ramon. We're doing just fine as we are."

I knew how he felt. I didn't want times to change either.

The phone rang.

"I'll get it!" Lizzy cried, lunging for the phone. "Coolidges . . . Dad! I knew it was you! Wait 'til you hear what happened in school today when—"

Catman kicked me under the table.

Ramon leaned in and whispered, "You should talk to your dad, Winnie."

They were right. If anything happened to Dad on the flight home and I'd refused to talk to him, I'd never forgive myself. Besides, I missed him. I missed his voice, the goofy look he got when he talked about his inventions. I even missed his dorky work suits.

I walked to the phone. Lizzy stopped in midsentence. "Dad! Winnie wants to talk to you!" She held the phone to my ear. Background laughter exploded over the receiver.

"Hi, Dad." My voice cracked.

"Winnie! Hey! How are you, honey?"

"Fine." He sounded a million miles away. "You?"

"Great! I wish you girls were here. The back bike is a big hit!" He said something else, but I lost it in the noise.

"Dad, when are you coming home?"

"What's that?" Dad asked.

In the background a woman's voice yelled, "Jack! Come on! We'll miss dinner!"

The receiver crackled. Dad called, away from the phone, "Be right there!"

Jack? Miss dinner? We'll miss dinner? I let go of the phone and backed away.

Lizzy caught the receiver and pulled it to her ear. "We love you too, Dad!" she shouted.

How could he? My heart raced and my head throbbed. I'd never missed Mom more than I did in that instant.

The rest of the meal was quiet, unless I just didn't hear the others. I wanted to escape to the barn, to bury my face in Nickers' fuzzy neck.

Finally the Colonel rose from the table. "We will take our leave. Ramon must finish his studies. And I have work to do before my men arrive—iron my uniform, spit-polish my boots!"

"You've spit-polished your boots every night of your life, Colonel," Bart observed.

The Colonel ignored his grandson and turned to Mrs. Coolidge. "A sheer delight, madame!"

Lizzy and I cleared the table, then sat down at it to do homework. I tried to read assigned poems, but they might as well have been math problems. I kept hearing *that woman's* voice: *Jack, we'll miss dinner.*

Lizzy yawned and packed up her books. "Let's tell the Coolidges good night and get some sleep. Where'd they go anyway?"

I shrugged.

Lightning flashed through the window. Thunder rumbled. The lights flickered.

Lizzy locked arms with me. "Let's find them!"

The house felt empty except for a few cats that scampered out of our way as we conducted a floor-by-floor search for the Coolidges.

"They can't just disappear!" Lizzy cried.

We started down from the third floor. Lightning lit up the sky outside the landing window. In the flash, I made out a human shape—on the roof.

"Lizzy!" I screamed. "Somebody's out there!"

The shape moved toward us, closer and closer to the window. Lizzy and I clutched each other. The window opened.

Catman stuck his head inside. He was standing on the roof, but he looked dry, in spite of the downpour. He motioned for us to come outside.

Lizzy and I exchanged glances, then climbed out. We followed Catman to a corner under one of the gables, where Mr. and Mrs. Coolidge sat on a plaid blanket.

Lightning flashed again, and they burst into applause. "Winnie! Lizzy!" called Mrs. Coolidge. She patted the blanket. We obeyed and sat down, joining their storm picnic. It seemed safe enough, with no metal in sight and the gable protecting us from the rain.

"Good one!" shouted Mr. Coolidge when the thunder rumbled long and loud.

They clapped for streaks of lightning. Catman snapped his fingers in his beatnik way of clapping.

"It's amazing!" Lizzy exclaimed, applauding. Then she burst out with a psalm I remembered our mom reading to us: *"God is our refuge and strength, always ready to help in times of trouble. So we will not fear, even if earthquakes come and the mountains crumble into the sea. Let the oceans roar and foam. Let the mountains tremble as the waters surge!"*

I leaned against the wall and watched lightning split the sky in jagged pieces. Thunder drummed all around us. Rain fell in sheets that sparkled in flashes of light that couldn't touch us.

I wondered if it could be raining in Chicago. Could Dad be watching rain and lightning? I wanted there to be some connection between his world and ours as I watched the nighttime show and listened to the Coolidges' cheers.

But it felt like Dad wasn't just in a different city. He was on some other planet, where even the rain and the lightning had different meanings. And the air we breathed couldn't possibly be the same.

Thursday morning I was a half second away
from getting another tardy from Ms. Brumby.
On Wednesday Mrs. Coolidge had used a
torture rod she called a curling iron to flip my
hair into a rolled-newspaper look. This morning,
while I'd eaten Frosted Flakes, she braided my
hair in dozens of tiny braids, which I unbraided
at the barn before I came to school. But it was
too late. The braids left me looking like a Dutch
Friesian—a stocky, European breed of horse with
a wild, bushy mane.

"Stick your finger in an electric socket?"
Summer asked as I slid into English class under
the bell. "You could be your own circus act!
Electric girl!"

Summer's faithful followers chuckled. Hawk

139

always sat by Summer in class, but I don't think she joined in. I was just glad we didn't have school on Friday. Maybe Mrs. Coolidge wouldn't feel obligated to fix my hair.

In Pat's class Barker asked for volunteers for the Ashland circus. "We need butchers—I mean, concession people—to sell cotton candy and peanuts."

"Come on, class!" Pat urged. "You could be circus folk like Barker!"

"Carny rats, more like it," Summer muttered. "No offense."

Summer Spidell is amazing. In the same breath she'd managed to insult Barker *and* make fun of Pat's "no offense" line.

I turned and gave Summer a disappointed look. "Bad news, Summer. That circus job you asked me about, it's a no-go."

Summer banged her desk. "I am *not* a fat lady!"

I acted puzzled. "Fat lady? You'll have to ask the Colonel about that job. I was talking about the *mean* lady. They said you were overqualified, but the job's filled. Maybe next year."

"Very funny!" Summer snapped. "Who'd want to be in that dirty, stinking circus anyway?"

Hawk raised her hand, and all heads turned

to her. "It would be my honor to be a greeter in the circus *and* a butcher, if that is all right."

"You got it!" Barker answered.

"Hawk!" Summer scolded.

I gave Hawk the thumbs-up. There was hope for that girl yet.

That night Hawk and I rode bareback to the fairgrounds, which had transformed into the Ashland circus. It was nice having Hawk around. Took my mind off the fact that Dad wasn't.

"But does the Colonel want me to be a greeter?" Hawk asked for the hundredth time. "Towaco doesn't know tricks like Nickers." It might have been the first time I'd seen Hawk nervous. She was even forgetting her perfect speech and slipping into contractions.

"You don't need tricks," I assured her. "The crowd just has to look at you!" Hawk had worn a buckskin dress, dignified Native American garb that worked perfectly with her Appaloosa. I wondered if her parents would make it to the circus. They're both lawyers, and I'd never seen either one of them at school stuff.

We led our horses to the Big Top and found Colonel Coolidge giving a pep talk to his volunteer butchers. Lizzy waved. About 20 kids, including Sal, Grant, M, and two Barker boys, were gathered around the Colonel.

"Lizzy!" Colonel Coolidge bellowed. "You and Mr. M are ticket takers!" He yawned. It looked out of place. He gave Grant and Sal coloring books. "Never forget there are 293 ways to make change for a dollar! Be vigilant!" Finally, he handed out peanut bags to a dozen kids. "Use the utmost caution! Peanuts are one of the ingredients of dynamite! And I want you people to polish your boots until they shine!"

I glanced at their feet. Every foot except the Colonel's was covered with a tennis shoe. And for the first time ever, Colonel Coolidge's boots looked muddy. He yawned again. He must have had a bad night. But I'd have bet money his boots would shine by the time his army buddies showed up Friday.

Catman must have noticed too. "Clean your boots for you, Colonel?"

The Colonel stared in horror at his boots. "I

polish my own boots, sir!" He did an about-face, shouted "Charge!" and then blew his ringmaster whistle.

Towaco followed Nickers in the parade. People cheered at Hawk on her Appaloosa. Nickers pranced, still wary of the noise and commotion. I waved to the crowd and spotted Pat Haven and Mr. Treadwater, my math teacher, and a bunch of people from church. The only one missing was Dad.

I stayed in the ring as long as I could to keep an eye on Ramon and Gabrielle. I didn't want anything to happen to either of them.

"Ladies and gentlemen!" The Colonel's voice over the mike drowned out everything else. "Welcome to Colonel Coolidge's Traveling Circus! I'd like to dedicate this evening's performance to the lovely Granny Barker!"

Catman met me as I led Nickers out of the ring. "Told you he had a thing for Ma Barker."

Hawk and I stabled our horses and rushed back to the Big Top in time to catch Barker's act. Catman and Matthew Barker had saved us seats, with Pat and Mrs. Barker farther down the row.

One by one, the Barker dogs trotted out and performed their tricks.

"Didn't Barker say at lunch that he was changing his act?" I whispered to Catman.

Catman pointed to the ring, where Bull, Matthew's bulldog, strolled out.

I elbowed Matthew. "You didn't tell us Bull was in the act!"

"Save the best for last!" he said, grinning in spite of himself.

"Another stray?" asked the Colonel. "Ladies and gentlemen, what should this master dog trainer teach *this* dog?"

I hoped it wouldn't be anything hard. Every time I'd seen Matthew's bulldog, it was sleeping. Barker admitted Bull was the laziest dog he'd ever seen.

While people in the crowd called out tricks, Bull turned in a circle and plopped down, his wrinkled head on his paws, his fat, stocky body still.

"Back flip!" shouted Jimmy Green Dingle-hopper, who was sitting two rows in front of us.

Back flip? Bull barely had a back!

I nudged Hawk. "See? He's trying to ruin Barker's act! No way Bull can do a flip!" Maybe I'd been right all along about Dinglehopper.

"Back flip?" Barker repeated, his voice cracking.

"Well, Master Trainer?" The Colonel tapped his foot. "We're waiting. Train this dog to do a back flip!"

The audience applauded. I wanted to clobber Dinglehopper with Matthew's cotton candy. He had to know that fat, lazy dog couldn't do a back flip!

Barker held his palms up in an I-give gesture. "Back flip, Bulldog!" he yelled.

Bull stood up, but that was all he did.

Matthew squirmed. I eyed the crowd and spotted Summer, smirking. She whispered something to Brian.

"Um . . . back flip!" Barker repeated. When Bull didn't respond, Barker stalled. He held up one finger, then combed his hair.

"We don't have all night!" barked the ringmaster. "I thought you could train any dog to do any trick. What about that back flip?"

I couldn't stand it. Poor Barker. And the Colonel wasn't helping.

Barker held up one finger, then bent to tie his shoelaces.

Bull came to life—at least for Bull. He trotted straight over to Barker and halfheartedly jumped up on him. The second Bull's paws hit Barker's legs, Eddy Barker stumbled and flipped Bull and himself over backwards in a perfect back flip.

"Back flip," Catman muttered.

"Way to go, Bull!" Matthew yelled.

"I'll be a monkey's uncle! No offense!" Pat exclaimed.

The crowd roared with laughter. I saw Brian clapping like crazy. Summer did her sissy two-fingers-on-palm clap.

Ramon and Midnight's act was next. As the crowd still roared with cheers for Barker the Master Dog Trainer, I got quiet, tuned out everything, and talked to God. *Please don't let anything bad happen to Midnight or Ramon. Keep them safe.*

I knew Lizzy would have said a lot more and said it better. But I loved the way God let me talk to him in the middle of a noisy circus. It felt like ducking under the corner gable in the middle of a rainstorm. Lizzy's storm verse popped into my head, the part about God being a refuge, a safe place to be even when the mountains were crumbling and the oceans roaring.

Catman and I moved down to watch ringside. Midnight galloped past us and into the ring as the Colonel asked the crowd to welcome "Ramon and his trick horse, Midnight Mystery."

For this act, Ramon wore a hidden microphone to interact with the audience. The stallion bowed, and Ramon dismounted. "Midnight, are you happy to see all these people?" he asked, as he did every performance.

But instead of the usual head-bob yes, Midnight shook his head no.

Ramon shifted his weight like a nervous American Saddle Horse. "Now Midnight, I think you misunderstood me." He went to his next question. "Is there any place in the world you'd rather be?"

Instead of answering *no,* Midnight bobbed *yes.*

"Something's wrong!" I told Catman.

"Tell the people how old you are, Midnight!" Ramon commanded.

But instead of pawing the ground, Midnight lay down.

Scattered laughter spread through the audience. I wanted to do something, but I couldn't think of any way to help.

Ramon got Midnight to his feet and tried again. But trick after trick got mixed up. Midnight missed every cue, and the spectators were laughing *at* Ramon, not with him.

Finally, the Colonel brought an end to the misery. "How about a hand for the independent thinker, Midnight Mystery!"

The crowd clapped politely, and Ramon, his face bright red, rode out of the ring.

"Catman," I said, trying to hold back my anger, "you know somebody's been messing with Midnight! He never would have missed all those cues on his own. Someone had to retrain him."

I remembered something Lizzy had told me Matthew Barker did once to his little brother William. Mrs. Barker had taught William the names of things like nose, mouth, ear. Then Matthew secretly *untrained* his brother. So one day when his mother asked, "William, where's your nose?" William pointed to his mouth. When she asked for "eye," he pointed to his nose. Matthew had been grounded until he got William straightened out again.

"That's it! Somebody taught Midnight the wrong cues!" I kicked the dirt in frustration.

"Two days ago I would have been convinced that Gabrielle LeBlond was behind this."

"Not now?" Catman asked.

"Well, of course not now! Gabrielle was a victim too. Remember? Somebody cut her surcingle. You saw it yourself." And Catman thought he was such a great detective!

He crooked his head for me to follow him. We were heading to the menagerie tent, but Catman couldn't just pass by the lion cages. He stopped and communed with his feline friends so long I almost went back to the Big Top. Finally he pulled himself away, and we slipped inside the animal tent.

He led me back to where the LeBlonds kept their tack. Gabrielle and her parents were back in the Big Top doing their acts, and we were the only humans there. Catman took down a white surcingle from a hook. The belt had been used, but it looked fairly new.

I shrugged. "So what? She got a new surcingle since hers was cut."

Catman patted my head. "Flash that photo of Gabrielle's *accident.*"

"I've told you, Catman! Photographic memory doesn't work that way. I can't control—!"

I stopped because for one of the rare times, a mental picture was coming when I really wanted it to. It was fuzzy, not perfect like the photos usually are. And it wasn't the broken surcingle or the accident. It was Gabrielle *before* the accident, showing her surcingle to Catman and me and bragging how *she* could perform without a saddle. But the surcingle in her hands had been *this* new-looking one, not the worn one Catman had picked up after Gabrielle's accident!

"Catman, why would Gabrielle practice with a new surcingle and perform with an old one? Unless she knew something was going to happen to it. . . . *She* did it herself! *She* cut the surcingle! She didn't want to ruin her good one, so she cut that old one! Gabrielle LeBlond faked her own accident!"

150

oy, did I underestimate Gabrielle!" I cried.
"She's meaner than Summer and twice as
sneaky!" I stormed out of the menagerie tent
and into the crowds pouring down the midway.
The circus must have ended. "Hurry, Catman!
We have to tell the Colonel!"

"Whoa!"

I stomped back to Catman. "Whoa? But
Gabrielle might get away! We have to tell the
Colonel—!"

"Chill, Winnie. I'll handle it."

"But—," I started to protest. I wanted to settle
everything right then and there. I wanted to see
the look on Gabrielle's face when she found out
we were onto her. But a lot of people were
about to be hurt. Ramon and the Colonel both

liked Gabrielle. And Gabrielle's parents? They'd be upset, too.

Maybe Catman was right. The Colonel was *his* great-grandfather, after all. He'd be the best one to break the news to him. Besides, it was late. I needed to get Nickers home. I longed to get her out of the circus and safe in her own barn.

"Okay, Catman. You handle it. I'm just glad we solved this thing before Ramon's big break." Now Ramon could forget about everything except the Clyde Beatty Cole Brothers Circus and putting on the cossack performance of his life.

Friday morning I woke up under a blanket of sadness. It was Mom's birthday. But she wasn't here. And neither was Dad. Lizzy tiptoed around the bedroom, getting ready for her writing competition trip, and I tried to go back to sleep. Being awake hurt too much.

I feel homesick, God, I prayed, snuggling up to Bumby, who purred on my pillow, his giant paws hanging off the edge. *I feel like a little kid*

*who wants her mommy and daddy. Why can't
things be like they used to be?*

I guess I did fall back to sleep because when I
woke up again sunshine filled the room and Lizzy
wasn't in it. She'd left me a note on the dresser:

*Winnie, we'll celebrate Mom's birthday as soon as
Dad gets back from Chicago. Try to have a good
day. God loves you, and so do I!!! Lizzy*

I got dressed and trudged downstairs.

On the kitchen table sat a big cake. On the
top of it Lizzy had written Mom's verse in bright
green frosting: *Jesus Christ is the same yesterday,
today, and forever.*

Pictures of Mom and her other birthday cakes
flooded my brain. But the kitchen was empty. The
whole world seemed empty. And yesterday,
today, and forever felt anything but "the same."

Bart Coolidge came thundering into the
kitchen. "Sa-a-ay! Cake for breakfast? I'll get the
tomato juice—Ohio's state drink! That reminds
me of a joke!"

As I walked to the barn early that afternoon, the
sky clouded in scallops, as if practicing for snow.

Nickers was as ready for a ride as I was. She nickered and pawed the dirt until I slipped on a hackamore and swung up bareback. I hugged her neck, smelling the clean horse scent, the pasture, and the earth. "Let's ride, girl."

We trotted out of town, cantered down country lanes, galloped on dirt paths. It felt as if we were the same being. Everything else disappeared. Every thought slipped from my mind, leaving nothing but the drum of hoofbeats and a sense of floating through time.

When we finally came back to the barn, Catman was waiting for us. "Almost time to split!" he called.

"You're kidding!" I called back. "What about Hawk?"

"Hawk's mom is driving Towaco." Catman pulled out a lunch bag.

Neither of Hawk's parents had made it to the circus the night before. I'd caught Hawk scanning the crowds for them all night. I was glad her mom was coming tonight.

Catman handed me a baloney sandwich when I dismounted. "The Colonel's invited us to the Kool-Aid toast."

I bit into the sandwich, suddenly realizing I

was starving. "At the Colonel's soldier reunion?" I felt honored . . . and a little scared.

"Right-on!" He picked up Burg and Moggie, two of his cats who must have followed him from home.

I picked up the brush and started in on Nickers' chest. "So how did the Colonel take it when you told him Gabrielle was the one sabotaging the circus?"

"Didn't," he answered.

"He didn't take it?"

"I didn't tell him."

"But you promised!" I shouted.

"I said I'd handle it," Catman reminded me. "I am."

"Catman!" I couldn't believe it. Calvin Catman Coolidge had chickened out! I should have done it myself. But I never in my wildest dreams thought he'd back out.

Catman was already starting to walk toward the fairgrounds. By the time I finished grooming Nickers, he and I had to trot to catch up with Catman.

"So what are you doing about Gabrielle?" I tried to control my temper, but I wasn't doing a good job. Nickers sensed my anger and didn't like it. She sidestepped nervously. I tried again, lowering my voice. "Did you at least talk to Gabrielle? Did she admit it?"

"Nope."

"She didn't admit it?"

"Didn't talk to her."

"You call that 'handling things'?" Did I have to do everything? Now I'd have to invade the Colonel's reunion to give him the bad news about Gabrielle. I didn't want to, but I had no choice. Who knew what Gabrielle had planned for Ramon tonight! And whether Jimmy Green Dinglehopper was in on it or not.

We walked through the circus parking lot, which was already half full. A white pickup truck with *Clyde Beatty Cole Brothers Circus* on the side was parked in the front row.

"Catman!" I exclaimed. "The scout's here! He really came! Give me two minutes to stable Nickers. Then you and I are going straight to the Colonel's trailer. And don't worry. I'll tell him about Gabrielle myself!"

Five minutes later we were at the door of the Colonel's trailer. I didn't want to go in. I'm lousy enough talking to people one-on-one. I wasn't looking forward to explaining everything to

Colonel Coolidge while his old army buddies listened on. I took a deep breath and knocked.

"Come in!" Ramon opened the door, and his smile faded. "Oh. Hi, Winnie. Thought you might be one of the Colonel's buddies."

"They're not here yet?" I glanced around the trailer. The canteens and a pitcher of grape Kool-Aid were set out on a table draped with an army blanket. The Colonel, dressed in his army uniform, paced in front of the table.

Ramon glanced nervously at him. "They probably had trouble finding Ashland, Colonel."

"Nonsense!" barked Colonel Coolidge. "My men can find an enemy bunker in an unmarked field in the middle of a blinding snowstorm! They'll be here!"

"Bad scene," Catman whispered. "Those cats should have been here by now."

Ramon shook his head. "I've never seen him like this. I don't know what he'll do if . . ."

The Colonel was muttering to himself. ". . . really give it to them for being late! . . . know better than to keep a superior officer waiting!"

I hated seeing him like that. But at least I wouldn't have to give him the bad news about Gabrielle with his buddies around. "Colonel

Coolidge?" I had to clear my throat. "I have to tell you something important. I've found out—"

He stopped pacing. "What? Do you know anything about this? Where are they? Did you see them out there?" He motioned toward the door. "Well?"

"No, sir!" My heart raced.

"Then why did you say you did?" he roared.

"But I didn't mean . . . I was just trying . . ." I couldn't get the words out.

Catman took my elbow and pulled me toward the door. "We'll go look for them, Colonel."

"Great idea!" Ramon agreed. "I'll stay here, you know, just in case they show up before you get back." He walked to the door with us. "Thanks." He lowered his voice. "A couple of the men are older than the Colonel. They really might be wandering around out there. Find them." He glanced over his shoulder at the Colonel, who was straightening his canteens. "Please."

Outside I turned on Catman. "I wanted to tell him about Gabrielle before his buddies get here, Catman!"

"*If* his buddies get here." He reached back and

158

tightened the rubber band on his blond ponytail, something I'd only seen him do when he was worried about something.

"What do you mean? Why wouldn't they come?" But as soon as I said it, I knew the only reason those men wouldn't come—sickness or death.

"You go that way." Catman pointed toward the midway. "I'll go this." He took out toward the Big Top.

I was glad I didn't have a watch. I knew we were running out of time. It was already starting to get dark. I wanted to find the Colonel's army buddies. We had to find them. I raced around the cotton-candy stand and bumped into somebody. "Sorry—"

"Hey! Watch it!"

I'd have recognized that snotty voice anywhere. Summer Spidell brushed off her black leather coat as if I'd spilled manure on her. She was flanked by two other girls from our class who had never spoken to me. "Winifred Willis. I might have known." Summer flipped her blonde hair over her shoulder. "If you're looking for your father, he went that way." She flicked her hand as if shooing flies.

"It wasn't *my* dad. He's in Chicago." I started to leave, but something stopped me.

Summer smirked at her buddies. "It's your dad all right. Didn't you know he was back?" She elbowed the girl in an identical leather coat. "And, Winnie, who's that woman he's with?"

Chapter

14

"You're lying!" I shouted at Summer. Why would she say she'd seen my dad with a woman? It was a new low, even for her.

Summer's smirk faded. "You really didn't know? I'm sorry, Winnie." Her pale blue eyes rounded, and she looked sorry for real. Summer Spidell, sorry for me?

I ran away as fast as I could. *She's wrong! Summer's a liar! Or she made a mistake.*

"Winnie!" Lizzy was running toward me, her shiny hair swaying. "We've been looking all over for you!" Breathless, she stopped in front of me. "Dad's here! He came back early to—!"

"Dad?" It was true?

Lizzy looked over her shoulder and waved.

Dad waved back wildly and trotted toward

us. And right behind him was a woman—tall, too tall, and too thin. She waved too.

"He shouldn't have bothered!" I screamed. I turned and ran the other way, ignoring their shouts, stumbling because I couldn't see, because everything looked blurry. Dad and a tall woman, on my mother's birthday!

I didn't stop running until I reached the Colonel's trailer. I stood on the step and wiped my tears with the back of my sleeve. *The same yesterday, today, and forever*? What a joke! Forget *about Dad. Just get through tonight. Help Ramon get through tonight.*

Ramon opened the trailer door. "Are you okay?"

"I'm fine!" I pushed past him. Catman was already back. I didn't see any old soldiers here, except the Colonel. He looked older, withered, as if his bones were dissolving.

"Ramon," I said, trying to control my shaky voice, "I know who's been sabotaging your act and trying to—"

The phone rang.

The Colonel snatched it before it stopped ringing. "Colonel Coolidge, 44th Division!" As he listened, his face changed, sagged like wax melting. He didn't speak for a long time. I saw him swallow. Then he turned his back to us. His shoulders slumped. At last he said, "Alden and Ayers too? . . . I understand. Thank you for calling, Mrs. House."

He hung up, and the click of the phone seemed as loud and final as thunder in the silent trailer. Slowly, as if he'd forgotten we were there, he walked to the table and fingered the three canteens on the end.

Ramon moved beside him. "Colonel?"

Colonel Coolidge took a deep breath and stood at attention. "Sergeant Alden, Private Ayers, and Second Lieutenant House will not be coming. They have gone to meet their maker. The world has not known better men."

I didn't know what to do. Tears burned my throat. Even Catman looked like he might cry, and I'd never seen him cry.

"I'm so sorry, Colonel." Ramon put his arm around the old man. They stood over the canteens, not speaking, just aching together. Finally Ramon spoke. "Colonel, let's cancel tonight's circus. I'll stay here with you and—"

Colonel Coolidge turned to face Ramon. "Cancel?"

"I think we should. We can give back gate money. It's no big deal."

"But the Beatty Show scout? He's out there."

Ramon shrugged. "We'll give him his money back too." He grinned, but I could tell how hard it was for him.

The Colonel took off his glasses, wiped them, and put them back on. "Ramon, you'd do that? Give up a chance at the Beatty Show?"

"Sure. I'd rather hang out with you tonight anyway."

Colonel Coolidge stared at Ramon. Then, as if something inside the broken man pulled together, he stood up straight and lifted his chin. "Not on your life! The show will go on! And you, Ramon, will put on the best performance of your career! You will show that scout what Ramon and Midnight Mystery can do! They will beg you to join their circus!" His voice softened. "And you will say yes."

Ramon shook his head. "But, Colonel—"

"That's an order, son." But he said it like a father, not a colonel.

The door opened, and in burst Gabrielle LeBlond. "What is with you people? You should

164

all be in the Big Top! Am I the only one around here who cares about the circus?"

Gabrielle! Having her barge in jarred me back to why I'd come to the Colonel's trailer in the first place. Her words echoed: *Am I the only one who cares about the circus?*

"You're the only one who *doesn't* care about the circus!" I shouted. I stormed over to her. "Gabrielle, we know everything. You might as well tell the truth. Admit to Ramon and the Colonel that you're responsible for Midnight's problems."

"Are you crazy?" She put her hands on her hips. "You saw for yourself last night! Somebody tried to ruin *my* act, too!"

"You did that yourself! *You* cut your old surcingle." I glanced to Catman to back me up, but he kept quiet. So I explained about the new surcingle and how Gabrielle had to have faked her own accident.

As I talked, Gabrielle's stone face softened. She looked away, then glared back at me. "So what! It's my surcingle anyway! I didn't hurt anybody but myself!"

"Gabrielle, why did you do it?" Ramon sounded hurt.

"Why? Because *she—*" she pointed to me—
"suspected *me!* Because I was sick of you getting
all the attention! Maybe I wanted people to
worry about me for a change."

"That doesn't excuse what you did to
Midnight and Ramon!" I insisted.

"I didn't do anything to Ramon!" Gabrielle
shouted. "Or his horse!"

"Pul-lease!" I shouted back. "Like we buy
that!"

"We buy that." Catman slipped in between
Gabrielle and me.

"What?" I couldn't believe him! And just
when I had Gabrielle cornered! When she was
about to confess! "Catman!" I whispered. "Leave
this to me!"

Catman ignored me and turned to the Colonel. "Colonel, why were your boots dirty yesterday? I know you polished them before you
went to bed. You can't sleep if your boots aren't
polished."

"Nonsense." But something flashed across the
Colonel's face. Fear?

"That blew my mind," Catman said. "Until I
saw what was on your boots. Manure. And
horsehair on your jacket. You got it retraining

166

Midnight in the middle of the night. That's why you yawned so much."

"Catman!" He *had* to be wrong. It didn't make any sense. But I remembered the dirty boots . . . and the yawning.

"Cut it out, Catman!" Ramon insisted. "The Colonel couldn't have done it!"

"Couldn't have given new cues from the ring with his ringmaster's whip?" Catman asked, not taking his gaze off the Colonel. "Put a burr under your blanket? Flashed the laser light? Put the wrong feed in the bin? Cut a hole in the lion cage?" Catman shook his head, and I could tell he would rather have been doing anything except this. "He could. He did. I just don't know why."

I stared at the Colonel, waiting for him to deny it. But he didn't.

"Colonel Coolidge did it?" Gabrielle repeated.

"Colonel?" Ramon's eyes pleaded with him. "Tell him he's wrong! Tell them you didn't do it!"

The Colonel hung his head. "I'm so sorry, Ramon. I—"

Ramon stepped back as if he'd been slapped. "How could you! I thought . . . I thought you cared for me! And all the time you only cared about your precious circus?"

"Ramon, please—" Colonel Coolidge reached for him, but Ramon stepped back.

"You never wanted me to have a chance with the big circus! And you knew how much it meant to me! That my mother—" Ramon broke off, choked with tears.

"No," the Colonel muttered, not looking up. "You don't understand. If I could take it back, I would!"

"Well you can't!" Ramon cried. "And here's a news flash for you! I quit!"

"Ramon, you can't quit yet!" roared the Colonel. "You have to ride tonight! The scout will—"

"Don't tell me what to do!" screamed Ramon. "Not anymore! Not ever!"

Catman ran his fingers through his hair. "Colonel, why did you do it? I know it's not just losing the act."

Someone knocked. We ignored it, but it got louder. Finally Gabrielle opened the door.

Dad stuck his head in. "Winnie! I want to talk to you!"

"Not now, Dad!" I whispered. The arguing had started back up, Ramon and the Colonel hurling words around the trailer so hard I wanted to duck.

"Come out, or I'm coming in," Dad said quietly. But I knew he meant it.

Gabrielle stepped aside, and I went out to Dad, pulling the door behind me. The angry voices leaked out, filling the air around us. "What?" I knew I sounded mean and hateful, but I didn't care. I peered behind him for the tall woman, but only Lizzy stood there, her eyes filled with tears.

"What's the matter with you, Winnie?" Dad asked. "I came back early to surprise you!"

I snorted. "I'm surprised all right! Who is she?"

"*She?* You mean Madeline? Is that what this is about?" He bit his cheek and got the look he gets when one of his inventions finally kicks in. "Winnie! You mean . . . you thought . . . ? Madeline's an inventor. I met her in Chicago. She lives in Loudonville! She had to leave the convention early, too. We agreed to meet here. I wanted her to meet you girls."

Dad sighed and scratched his head, like he was as mixed up about it as I was. Softly, he admitted, maybe just now admitting it to himself, "She makes me laugh, Winnie. It's been a long time since that happened."

Lizzy sniffled, still shaking from crying.

Dad leaned down and hugged me, but I couldn't hug him back. My arms and legs felt like tree trunks. I wanted to run away, to escape inside the warmth of my barn, where none of this could touch me.

Are you listening, God? I prayed. I closed my eyes and waited. *I need you! I don't know what to do or think. I want things to be the way they used to be.* Everything faded—the shouting inside the trailer, the noise of the midway, Lizzy's crying. It felt like I'd stepped inside a safe place, like Pat's Pets on a cold day or the corner of the Coolidge roof, where storms were applauded and not feared. A shelter. A refuge.

In my mind, I could see my mom holding her birthday cake, the green letters spelling out her verse from Hebrews. I read it again, and this time the beginning jumped at me: Jesus Christ *is the same yesterday, today, and forever.*

I let the words soak into my veins and travel to my heart. *Is that it, Lord?* You're *the same! Even if nothing else is, you are?* I wanted to stay angry. It wasn't enough. But I thought about how many times in the last few days I'd felt like I was losing it. And each time I'd remembered to duck in and pray, God had been there waiting—in Coolidge Castle, in school, in the circus.

I still wanted things to be the same. I wanted Mom back. I didn't want Dad to go to conventions or meet women inventors. But no matter what happened, I'd always have this refuge to come to. And I had a feeling that would be enough.

My arms were thawing, melting into my dad. I hugged him back. "I'm sorry, Dad."

Lizzy threw her arms around my neck. "Winnie, I've been so worried about you!"

I smiled at my sister and turned back to Dad. "I didn't want you to go to Chicago, Dad. I was afraid something would happen to you, that you wouldn't come home."

"Winnie! I couldn't stand spending another day away from you girls!"

I laughed. "I think I would have done anything to keep you home. . . ." I stopped. I could almost feel my brain cells piecing things together. "That's it! I get it now! Dad, Lizzy, we're okay, really! I have to talk to the Colonel."

"Can we do anything, honey?" Dad asked.

I hugged him again. "Go get a good seat! I'll see you in the Big Top!"

They left, and I went back inside the trailer. Gabrielle was still standing by the door. "Gabrielle, I'm sorry I thought you were the one doing everything," I whispered.

The Colonel was sitting by the canteens, his head in his hands. Ramon towered over him, looking like he'd moved right past anger and straight into hurt.

Everybody, even Gabrielle, turned to stare at me. I cleared my throat. "Colonel, I understand why you did what you did."

Ramon glared at me. "How can you say that? He's a selfish old man who doesn't care about anything except his circus!"

I shook my head. "He just didn't want things to change."

Colonel Coolidge glanced up at me, and I knew I was right. "You couldn't stand the thought of losing Ramon, could you, Colonel? You did all those things to Ramon and Midnight because you wanted things to stay the same. Tell him."

He nodded.

"Of course he didn't want things to change!" shouted Ramon. "He had to keep the cossack act for his own circus."

I shook my head. "Ramon, the Colonel wasn't afraid of losing your act. He was afraid of losing *you!*"

Ramon studied the Colonel. "Me?"

The Colonel's voice shook when he finally spoke. "I like homeschooling you. I like having breakfast together. Talking about the circus. Watching how you are with people. Ramon, I *am* a selfish old man. I didn't want to lose you. But after tonight . . . you have to believe me. I wouldn't have done anything to hurt your chances with the Beatty scout! Can you forgive me?"

"He did tell you to go ahead with the act. Remember, Ramon?" Catman said.

Ramon hadn't moved.

Tears filled the Colonel's eyes. "I'm an old fool, Ramon."

I walked over to them. "Ramon, the Colonel was scared. He loves you so much. He was afraid you'd leave and forget about him."

Ramon gazed out the window as if he were watching a whole circus perform outside. Then he stared down at the Colonel. "How could anybody forget Colonel Coolidge?" Ramon asked. A hint of a smile flashed in his eyes.

"Better men than I have tried." He held out his hand, and the Colonel took it.

Gabrielle turned toward the door. "This is all very touching. But we have a show to put on!" Some of the bite had gone out of her, and I thought I saw her wipe away a tear.

"Wait!" commanded the Colonel. "Gabrielle, we need a little something extra for our final performance. I don't suppose you could pull together that dancing-horse act?"

"Are you kidding?" she shouted, a smile breaking over her whole face. "I've been ready my whole life!"

The Colonel jumped to his feet. "Ramon, get a move on! You have to get ready!"

"Colonel!" Ramon held up his hand. For a minute I was afraid he was really quitting. "We have a toast to perform first. The show can wait."

Ramon poured Kool-Aid into the Colonel's canteen while Catman and I turned the other three canteens upside down. Then Colonel Coolidge drank a solemn toast to his men.

When he set down his canteen, the Colonel turned to Ramon. "On with the show!"

174

Pat Haven and Hawk had Nickers ready for me under the Big Top. Lizzy had told them at least part of what was going on. She and Dad were waiting at the entrance with the tall woman.

Dad's eyebrows arched like they do when he's afraid I'm going to go crazy. "Winnie, this is Madeline Edison, just about the best inventor at the convention."

"Hardly," she said. "Glad to meet you, Winnie. Your dad talks about you all the time."

I nodded, trying to think of something to say. But I couldn't. Poor Dad would have to settle for my attempt at a smile.

The whistle blew, and they left for the bleachers.

Hawk and I stayed together for the little bit of greeting time left. In between greetings, I filled Hawk in. She didn't say much, didn't judge me or tell me I was stupid for worrying about losing my dad. It made me wish I'd talked to her sooner.

The Colonel dedicated the last performance to the men of the Fighting 44th, and it was the best show ever. Ramon's cossack act brought the crowd to its feet, cheering wildly as Ramon performed every stunt to perfection. Midnight had never looked more beautiful.

At the end of the act, the Colonel shouted into the microphone, "You have just seen Ramon and the Magnificent Midnight Mystery! They are undoubtedly the finest cossack act in the business! Any circus would be lucky to have this dynamic duo!"

I had no doubts that the Clyde Beatty Cole Brothers Circus would agree. I didn't know if Ramon would take the job or stay with the Colonel. But I knew they'd both be okay. They loved each other, and that wasn't about to change.

After the last act, the Colonel asked the crowd to applaud and bring back the performers for a final bow. Hawk and I grabbed Towaco and Nickers and ran to the ring.

I hugged Nickers, feeling safe, loving her so much it hurt. I swung up on her back and stared at the crowd. Pat waved at us. And so did the Barkers and Coolidges. Catman stood ringside, his fingers forming a *V* for victory. Seeing these friends I hadn't even met six months before made me think that maybe some changes *were* okay.

I swept my arm in front of me and gave Nickers the cue to bow. And as if she'd been doing it her whole life, she tucked her leg under her and lowered her head, making the most beautiful bow any horse had ever made.

Ramon gave me a thumbs-up. I grinned at Lizzy and Dad, who were on their feet, cheering.

And as Nickers bowed low, something inside of me bowed too.

The whole circus felt better than the greatest show on earth. It was a giant birthday party for my mother.

I bowed my head and closed my eyes. "Happy birthday, Mom!"

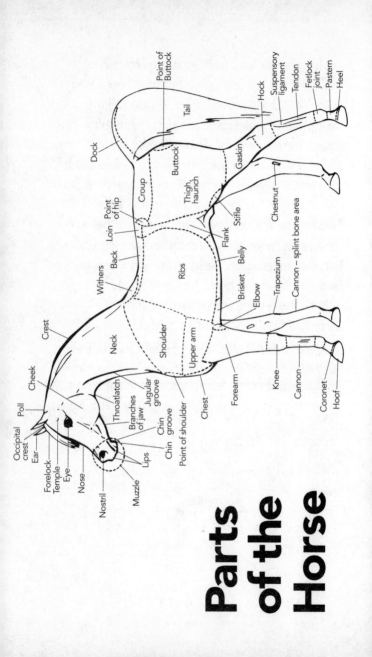

Parts of the Horse

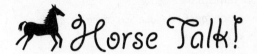 Horse Talk!

Horses communicate with one another . . . and with us, if we learn to read their cues. Here are some of the main ways a horse talks:

Whinny—A loud, long horse call that can be heard from a half mile away. Horses often whinny back and forth.
Possible translations: *Is that you over there? Hello! I'm over here! See me? I heard you! What's going on?*

Neigh—To most horse people, a neigh is the same as a whinny. Some people call any vocalization from a horse a neigh.

Nicker—The friendliest horse greeting in the world. A nicker is a low sound made in the throat, sometimes rumbling. Horses use it as a warm greeting for another horse or a trusted person. A horse owner might hear a nicker at feeding time.
Possible translations: *Welcome back! Good to see you. I missed you. Hey there! Come on over. Got anything good to eat?*

Snort—This sounds like your snort, only much louder and more fluttering. It's a hard exhale, with the air being forced out through the nostrils.

Possible translations: *Look out! Something's wrong out there! Yikes! What's that?*

Blow—Usually one huge exhale, like a snort, but in a large burst of wind.

Possible translations: *What's going on? Things aren't so bad. Such is life.*

Squeal—This high-pitched cry that sounds a bit like a scream can be heard a hundred yards away.

Possible translations: *Don't you dare! Stop it! I'm warning you! I've had it—I mean it! That hurts!*

Grunts, groans, sighs, sniffs—Horses make a variety of sounds. Some grunts and groans mean nothing more than boredom. Others are natural outgrowths of exercise.

★★★★★

Horses also communicate without making a sound. You'll need to observe each horse and tune in to the individual translations, but here are some possible versions of nonverbal horse talk:

EARS

Flat back ears—When a horse pins back its ears, pay attention and beware! If the ears go back slightly, the horse may just be irritated. The closer the ears are pressed back to the skull, the angrier the horse.

Possible translations: *I don't like that buzzing fly. You're making me mad! I'm warning you! You try that, and I'll make you wish you hadn't!*

Pricked forward, stiff ears—Ears stiffly forward usually mean a horse is on the alert. Something ahead has captured its attention.

Possible translations: *What's that? Did you hear that? I want to know what that is! Forward ears may also say, I'm cool and proud of it!*

Relaxed, loosely forward ears—When a horse is content, listening to sounds all around, ears relax, tilting loosely forward.

Possible translations: *It's a fine day, not too bad at all. Nothin' new out here.*

Uneven ears—When a horse swivels one ear up and one ear back, it's just paying attention to the surroundings.

Possible translations: *Sigh. So, anything interesting going on yet?*

Stiff, twitching ears—If a horse twitches stiff ears, flicking them fast (in combination with overall body tension), be on guard! This horse may be terrified and ready to bolt.

Possible translations: *Yikes! I'm outta here! Run for the hills!*

Airplane ears—Ears lopped to the sides usually means the horse is bored or tired.
Possible translations: Nothing ever happens around here. So, what's next already? Bor-ing.

Droopy ears—When a horse's ears sag and droop to the sides, it may just be sleepy, or it might be in pain.
Possible translations: Yawn . . . I am so sleepy. I could sure use some shut-eye. I don't feel so good. It really hurts.

TAIL

Tail switches hard and fast—An intensely angry horse will switch its tail hard enough to hurt anyone foolhardy enough to stand within striking distance. The tail flies side to side and maybe up and down as well.
Possible translations: I've had it, I tell you! Enough is enough! Stand back and get out of my way!

Tail held high—A horse who holds its tail high may be proud to be a horse!
Possible translations: Get a load of me! Hey! Look how gorgeous I am! I'm so amazing that I just may hightail it out of here!

Clamped-down tail—Fear can make a horse clamp its tail to its rump.
Possible translations: I don't like this; it's scary. What are they going to do to me? Can't somebody help me?

Pointed tail swat—One sharp, well-aimed swat of the tail could mean something hurts there.

Possible translations: *Ouch! That hurts! Got that pesky fly.*

OTHER SIGNALS

Pay attention to other body language. Stamping a hoof may mean impatience or eagerness to get going. A rear hoof raised slightly off the ground might be a sign of irritation. The same hoof raised, but relaxed, may signal sleepiness. When a horse is angry, the muscles tense, back stiffens, and the eyes flash, showing extra white of the eyeballs. One anxious horse may balk, standing stone still and stiff legged. Another horse just as anxious may dance sideways or paw the ground. A horse in pain might swing its head backward toward the pain, toss its head, shiver, or try to rub or nibble the sore spot. Sick horses tend to lower their heads and look dull, listless, and unresponsive.

As you attempt to communicate with your horse and understand what he or she is saying, remember that different horses may use the same sound or signal, but mean different things. One horse may flatten her ears in anger, while another horse lays back his ears to listen to a rider. Each horse has his or her own language, and it's up to you to understand.

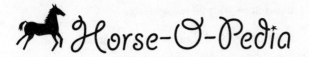

Horse-O-Pedia

American Saddlebred (or American Saddle Horse)—A showy breed of horse with five gaits (walk, trot, canter, and two extras). They are usually high-spirited, often high-strung; mainly seen in horse shows.

Andalusian—A breed of horse originating in Spain, strong and striking in appearance. They have been used in dressage, as parade horses, in the bullring, and even for herding cattle.

Appaloosa—Horse with mottled skin and a pattern of spots, such as a solid white or brown with oblong, dark spots behind the withers. They're usually good all-around horses.

Arabian—Believed to be the oldest breed or one of the oldest. Arabians are thought by many to be the most beautiful of all horses. They are characterized by a small head, large eyes, refined build, silky mane and tail, and often high spirits.

Barb—North African desert horse.

Bay—A horse with a mahogany or deep brown to reddish-brown color and a black mane and tail.

Blind-age—Without revealing age.

Brumby—A bony, Roman-nosed, Australian scrub horse, disagreeable and hard to train.

Buck—To thrust out the back legs, kicking off the ground.

Buckskin—Tan or grayish-yellow-colored horse with black mane and tail.

Canter—A rolling-gait with a three time pace slower than a gallop. The rhythm falls with the right hind foot, then the left hind and right fore simultaneously, then the left fore followed by a period of suspension when all feet are off the ground.

Cattle-pony stop—Sudden, sliding stop with drastically bent haunches and rear legs; the type of stop a cutting, or cowboy, horse might make to round up cattle.

Chestnut—A horse with a coat colored golden yellow to dark brown, sometimes the color of bays, but with same-color mane and tail.

Cloverleaf—The three-cornered racing pattern followed in many barrel races; so named because the circles around each barrel resemble the three petals on a clover leaf.

Clydesdale—A very large and heavy draft breed. Clydesdales have been used for many kinds of work, from towing barges along canals, to plowing fields, to hauling heavy loads in wagons.

Colic—A digestive disorder in horses, accompanied by severe abdominal pain.

Conformation—The overall structure of a horse; the way his parts fit together. Good conformation in a horse means that horse is solidly built, with straight legs and well-proportioned features.

Crop—A small whip sometimes used by riders.

Cross-ties—Two straps coming from opposite walls of the stallway. They hook onto a horse's halter for easier grooming.

Curb—A single-bar bit with a curve in the middle and shanks and a curb chain to provide leverage in a horse's mouth.

D ring—The D-shaped, metal ring on the side of a horse's halter.

Dutch Friesian—A stocky, large European breed of horses who have characteristically bushy manes.

English Riding—The style of riding English or Eastern or Saddle Seat, on a flat saddle that's lighter and leaner than a Western saddle. English riding is seen in three-gaited and five-gaited Saddle Horse classes in horse shows. In competition, the rider posts at the trot and wears a formal riding habit.

Gait—Set manner in which a horse moves. Horses have four natural gaits: the walk, the trot or jog, the canter or lope, and the gallop. Other gaits have been learned or are characteristic to certain breeds: pace, amble, slow gait, rack, running walk, etc.

Gelding—An altered male horse.

Hackamore—A bridle with no bit, often used for training Western horses.

Halter—Basic device of straps or rope fitting around a horse's head and behind the ears. Halters are used to lead or tie up a horse.

Hunter—A horse used primarily for hunt riding. Hunter is a type, not a distinct breed. Many hunters are bred in Ireland, Britain, and the U.S.

Leadrope—A rope with a hook on one end to attach to a horse's halter for leading or tying the horse.

Leads—The act of a horse galloping in such a way as to balance his body, leading with one side or the other. In a *right lead*, the right foreleg leaves the ground last and seems to reach out farther. In a *left lead*, the horse reaches out farther with the left foreleg, usually when galloping counterclockwise.

Lipizzaner—Strong, stately horse used in the famous Spanish Riding School of Vienna. Lipizzaners are born black and turn gray or white.

Lunge line (longe line)—A very long lead line or rope, used for exercising a horse from the ground. A hook at one end of the line is attached to the horse's halter, and the horse is encouraged to move in a circle around the handler.

Lusitano—Large, agile, noble breed of horse from Portugal. They're known as the mounts of bullfighters.

Mare—Female horse.

Maremmano—A classical Greek warhorse descended from sixteenth-century Spain. It was the preferred mount of the Italian cowboy.

Morgan—A compact, solidly built breed of horse with muscular shoulders. Morgans are usually reliable, trustworthy horses.

Mustang—Originally, a small, hardy Spanish horse turned loose in the wilds. Mustangs still run wild in protected parts of the U.S. They are suspicious of humans, tough, hard to train, but quick and able horses.

Paddock—Fenced area near a stable or barn; smaller than a pasture. It's often used for training and working horses.

Paint—A spotted horse with Quarter Horse or Thoroughbred bloodlines. The American Paint Horse Association registers only those horses with Paint, Quarter Horse, or Thoroughbred registration papers.

Palomino—Cream-colored or golden horse with a silver or white mane and tail.

Palouse—Native American people who inhabited the Washington–Oregon area. They were hightly skilled in horse training and are credited with developing the Appaloosas.

Percheron—A heavy, hardy breed of horse with a good disposition. Percherons have been used as elegant draft horses, pulling royal coaches. They've also been good workhorses on farms. Thousands of Percherons from America served as warhorses during World War I.

Pinto—Spotted horse, brown and white or black and white. Refers only to color. The Pinto Horse Association registers any spotted horse or pony.

Post—A riding technique in English horsemanship. The

rider posts to a rising trot, lifting slightly out of the saddle and back down, in coordination with the horse's bounciest gait, the trot.

Przewalski—Perhaps the oldest breed of primitive horse. Also known as the Mongolian Wild Horse, the Przewalski Horse looks primitive, with a large head and a short, broad body.

Quarter Horse—A muscular "cowboy" horse reminiscent of the Old West. The Quarter Horse got its name from the fact that it can outrun other horses over the quarter mile. Quarter Horses are usually easygoing and good-natured.

Quirt—A short-handled rawhide whip sometimes used by riders.

Rear—To suddenly lift both front legs into the air and stand only on the back legs.

Roan—The color of a horse when white hairs mix with the basic coat of black, brown, chestnut, or gray.

Snaffle—A single bar bit, often jointed, or "broken" in the middle, with no shank. Snaffle bits are generally considered less punishing than curbed bits.

Sorrel—Used to describe a horse that's reddish (usually reddish-brown) in color.

Spur—A short metal spike or spiked wheel that straps to the heel of a rider's boots. Spurs are used to urge the horse on faster.

Stallion—An unaltered male horse.

Standardbred—A breed of horse heavier than the Thoroughbred, but similar in type. Standardbreds have a calm temperament and are used in harness racing.

Surcingle—A type of cinch used to hold a saddle, blanket, or a pack to a horse. The surcingle looks like a wide belt.

Tack—Horse equipment (saddles, bridles, halters, etc.).

Tennessee Walker—A gaited horse, with a running walk—half walk and half trot. Tennessee Walking Horses are generally steady and reliable, very comfortable to ride.

Thoroughbred—The fastest breed of horse in the world, they are used as racing horses. Thoroughbreds are often high-strung.

Tie short—Tying the rope with little or no slack to prevent movement from the horse.

Trakehner—Strong, dependable, agile horse that can do it all—show, dressage, jump, harness.

Twitch—A device some horsemen use to make a horse go where it doesn't want to go. A rope noose loops around the upper lip. The loop is attached to what looks like a bat, and the bat is twisted, tightening the noose around the horse's muzzle until he gives in.

Welsh Cob—A breed of pony brought to the U.S. from the United Kingdom. Welsh Cobs are great all-around ponies.

Western Riding—The style of riding as cowboys of the Old West rode, as ranchers have ridden, with a traditional Western saddle, heavy, deep-seated, with a raised saddle horn. Trail riding and pleasure riding are generally Western; more relaxed than English riding.

Wind sucking—The bad, and often dangerous, habit of some stabled horses to chew on fence or stall wood and suck in air.

 # Author Talk

Dandi Daley Mackall grew up riding horses, taking her first solo bareback ride when she was three. Her best friends were Sugar, a Pinto; Misty, probably a Morgan; and Towaco, an Appaloosa; along with Ash Bill, a Quarter Horse; Rocket, a buckskin; Angel, the colt; Butch, anybody's guess; Lancer and Cindy, American Saddlebreds; and Moby, a white Quarter Horse. Dandi and husband, Joe; daughters, Jen and Katy; and son, Dan (when forced) enjoy riding Cheyenne, their Paint. Dandi has written books for all ages, including Little Blessings books, Degrees of Guilt: *Kyra's Story*, Degrees of Betrayal: *Sierra's Story*, *Love Rules*, and *Maggie's Story*. Her books (about 400 titles) have sold more than 4 million copies. She writes and rides from rural Ohio.

Visit Dandi at www.dandibooks.com

Coming in 2008!

Starlight Animal Rescue

A new series by Dandi Daley Mackall

Not so far away from Winnie and Nickers is an amazing place called Starlight Animal Rescue, headed by none other than Catman's cousin, who frequently e-mails the Pet Help Line and Winnie for horse-gentling tips. The rescue is a farm where hopeless horses are loved and trained, where discarded dogs become heroes, where stray cats are transformed into trusted companions, and where troubled teens find help through the animals they rescue.

A sneak peek at Book 1, *Runaway* . . .

I've run away seven times—

never once to anything, just away from.

Maybe that's why they call me a "runaway"

and not a "run-to."

Meet Dakota Brown, who used to love all things "horse" until she lost everything, including hope. The minute she sets foot in the Starlight Animal Rescue, she plans her escape. But can an "impossible" horse named Blackfire and this odd collection of quirky animal lovers be the home she's always dreamed of?

Winnie
The Horse Gentler

1 **WILD THING**

2 **EAGER STAR**

3 **BOLD BEAUTY**

4 **MIDNIGHT MYSTERY**

5 **UNHAPPY APPY**

6 **GIFT HORSE**

7 **FRIENDLY FOAL**

8 **BUCKSKIN BANDIT**

COLLECT ALL EIGHT BOOKS!

Winnie
The Horse Gentler

Can't get enough of Winnie? Visit her Web site to read more about Winnie and her friends plus all about their horses.

IT'S ALL ON WINNIETHEHORSEGENTLER.COM
There are so many fun and cool things to do on Winnie's Web site; here are just a few:

 PAT'S PETS
Post your favorite photo of your pet and tell us a fun story about them

 ASK WINNIE
Here's your chance to ask Winnie questions about your horse

MANE ATTRACTION
Meet Dandi and her horse, Chestnut!

 THE BARNYARD
Here's your chance to share your thoughts with others

AND MUCH MORE!